The Deadly Tapestry

Tangled Threads Mysteries
Book 1

Ellie Webster

Liquid Mind Publishing
This is a work of fiction. All characters, names, places and events are the product of the author's imagination or used fictitiously.

Tangled Threads Mysteries

The Deadly Tapestry

A Stitch Too Far

Join Ellie Webster's Newsletter

Follow the link to join our newsletter and stay up to date with upcoming releases, deals, and exclusive cozy content!

https://www.getdrip.com/forms/99805461/submissions/new

TANGLED THREADS SERIES

THE *Deadly* TAPESTRY

ELLIE WEBSTER

Chapter 1

A Cryptic Message

"Come on, Mewsly. It's clean-up time."

Maisie Button gently lifted the yawning, round tabby cat off the farmhouse table at the front of her shop. Mewsly, her green-gold eyes barely open, chirped in protest as she was removed from the bright patch of spring sunlight and set down on the wooden floor.

"You have plenty of places to nap," Maisie reminded her as she tucked a stray strand of auburn hair back into her loose bun and pushed up the sleeves of her cardigan. Outside, the evening sky was settling into a soft grey, and a gentle spring drizzle pattered against the windows, carrying the scent of new leaves. "It's almost time for our friends to get here."

Her collection of bracelets jangling, Maisie reached across the tabletop to gather up all the items that customers had left behind in the store that day. Three rolls of fabric, a pair of knitting needles, an empty coffee mug, a couple of fat quarter-yards of fabric cut into squares, and a handful of loose buttons in various shapes and sizes.

Her Knit and Natter group were due to arrive at six o'clock, and she wanted to spruce the place up before they got here.

Maisie hummed quietly to herself as she put the buttons in the "Mix and Match" drawer. Every child who visited Tangled Threads made a beeline for that drawer, until they spotted Mewsly. Or decided to try out the rocking chair in the corner, which was draped with a soft, hand-woven cotton throw in cheerful colors and couldn't have looked more inviting. Or the jar of free marshmallows Maisie kept at her beverage station, where she offered her customers freshly brewed coffee, fragrant teas, or a warm cup of hot chocolate—perfect for an April day when the weather couldn't quite make up its mind.

Tangled Threads had been the center of forty-four-year-old Maisie's life since she'd moved to Thistle Grove ten months ago. The slow pace of the store was worlds away from her old life in LA, where she'd worked long hours on set as a costume designer.

Maisie smiled at the small photograph she kept in a frame by the cash register. She'd been married then, too, to Frank, a career cameraman with warm brown eyes a shade lighter than her own and an accidental soulful sweep of brown hair across his brow.

Their life together with Mewsly, their first and only "baby," had been a seesaw of weeks away on location and giddy, crammed-in fun when the stars and their calendars aligned. His sudden death at the hands of a drunk driver had ripped her life apart at the seams. Nothing was the same after that.

It was hard to believe that this summer, she and Mewsly would be celebrating their one-year anniversary as residents of this tiny town in the Willamette Valley in her home state of Oregon. An occasion that would no doubt call for cake and coffee.

She smirked. Then again, most days at Tangled Threads included some kind of sweet treat, and every day, rain or shine, there was hot coffee in the pot.

Maisie glanced around her store and felt a soft glow of pride settle over her. This was it, her fresh start, and she'd built a warm, welcoming community around the craft shop.

Tangled Threads sat at the far end of Main Street, tucked between Dillard's Bakehouse and Turn the Page Used Books. Just a few doors down, the bustle of cafés and little shops gave way to cozy weatherboard houses and back gardens shaded by tall Douglas firs.

In the window stood a sassy, faceless mannequin with her hand on her hip, nicknamed Vivienne after Maisie's favorite designer. She'd brought it with her from L.A.

Vivienne wore a flowing purple gypsy skirt, a light embroidered blouse, and a beaded satchel dangled from her shoulder. A tad different to the elaborate costumes Maisie had used her to work on in the movie world.

Of course, the patterns for all the clothes were prominently displayed at her tip-toed feet. A basket beside her held soft cotton yarns in fresh pastel shades, with a few knitting needles arranged playfully among them, and a sign on the glass invited passersby to stop in for a coffee and a browse.

Inside the store, customers were greeted by a cubbyhole display along the righthand wall of the shop, stuffed with skeins and hanks of yarn, fine and chunky, natural and acrylic, in a bright array of colors. Standing beside it was an antique bookcase repurposed as a button and bead display. Open glass jars lined the shelves, full of assorted treasures in all shapes and sizes.

The bottom shelf had been fashioned into a drawer with a plexiglass front labelled *Mix and Match*. Inside were the hundreds of random buttons, beads, and the occasional marble that Maisie had collected from her work in L.A., as well as the garage sales and craft fairs she'd visited on her travels.

Then came the fabric. Stacks of fat quarters in a wire display and a stand of flannels, ginghams, cottons, and silks rolled into tight bolts. Drawers full of patterns took up the last few feet of space along the wall, labelled as *Adults or Children, Tops or Bottoms, Eveningwear, Swimwear*, or *Accessories*.

Maisie loved browsing the different colors, textures and weaves in the material. Textiles were in her blood, and in her quieter, more reflective moments, she took out her photo album that she kept in the back of the store and paged through the pictures of all the costumes she'd designed over the course of her Hollywood career.

The lefthand side of the shop featured a large, rustic farmhouse table, a space specifically for sitting, talking and crafting. The seating was a mix of styles, from an old kitchen chair painted bright yellow to a wooden barstool with a purple cushion and everything in between. When she'd arrived in town, she'd collected what she could, but the eclectic mix kind of worked, so she hadn't changed it.

On the wall above the table hung the Tangled Threads Brag Board, a rectangular corkboard where customers could tack up photos of finished projects they were particularly proud of. Beside it was Maisie's coffee station, a side table with a double-burner coffee maker and jars of tea bags, hot chocolate mix, and marshmallows.

The rocking chair was set a few feet away, next to a stack of well-thumbed craft magazines. It was her favorite place to while away a few spare hours, getting inspiration and ideas, and catching up on the recent trends.

Finally, behind the counter, through an open doorway, was her back-room office. In it was a worn wooden desk that she'd found at an antique show, and filing cabinet for her paperwork. A small, attached kitchenette let her prepare snacks, store her lunch and, of course, feed Mewsly.

The cat, unwilling to let her eviction go unprotested, had planted herself on the floor by the table and begun a thorough cleaning of her back paw. She was five years old and a classic mackerel tabby—black stripes and markings over shades of warm grey, russet brown, and beige the color of milky tea.

Maisie smiled fondly as she thought back to how Frankie had found her in a box as a tiny kitten, stashed beside a dumpster. He'd brought her home and from the moment Maisie had seen her little, furry head and big, round eyes, the tabby had stolen her heart.

Knowing she was being thought about, Mewsly meowed as Maisie passed by with the empty coffee mugs and tried to weave between her legs.

"Honestly, Mewsly, one of these days I'm going to tread on you, if you're not careful."

The cat ran ahead of her into the kitchenette, her fluffy underbelly wobbling, and stared at her empty food dish.

"Absolutely not. You had dinner half an hour ago, remember?"

Maisie washed out the empty mugs and glanced at the

clock on the wall. In a few minutes, the first Thistle Grove locals would arrive, armed with their current projects.

The Friday Knit and Natter Nights had been the first event Maisie had set up after moving to Thistle Grove and opening the store. It had soon been followed by Sew Something on Saturday mornings and seasonal promotions like Craft Your Heart Out on Valentine's Day and Spooky Specials on Halloween.

A budding social life had soon followed, and Maisie felt lucky to have made such warm and welcoming friends in her new hometown. With the weekly knitting circle had come a colorful cast of friendly and fiercely loyal fellow creatives, even if they were a little heavy-handed with Mewsly's cat treats.

She pulled a wooden chopping board out from one of the kitchen drawers and laid out a fresh gingerbread loaf that she'd baked at home and brought with her. Mewsly watched as she cut it into thick slices.

Mewsly nudged her leg.

"It is nice, isn't it?" she said with a proud smile. At first, she'd taken up baking to pass the time when she'd first moved to Thistle Grove, but to her surprise, she'd really enjoyed it. It was a bit like sewing in that it required precision, concentration, and attention to detail. "Let's hope it tastes as good as it looks."

Next on the prep list was coffee. Maisie always had a pot brewing for any customer who wanted a cup to browse with, but for Knit and Natter nights, she liked to make something special. On offer this evening would be hazelnut roast and regular half-caf, for anyone who liked a late beverage but still wanted to sleep.

The bell over the shop door jangled, and Maisie poked her head out of the kitchenette.

"Hello, Ree!" She waved at the retired schoolteacher. Iris "Ree" Davenport was a slender woman in her seventies with long, white hair that she wore in a braid over one shoulder.

"Hi, Maisie," Ree called back. After years of stitching costumes for school plays, she now spent her days happily knitting and quilting—hobbies she'd finally had time to indulge in once she retired.

As a costume designer, Maisie had never worked much with quilts, so she loved having Ree's gentle expertise on all things batting and backing. Like the baking, she enjoyed the challenge of quilting and was even considering sponsoring a quilting competition later in the year. Apparently, there'd used to be one, but it had ceased when the hosts had moved out of the area some years ago.

Ree took her usual seat at the crafting table and set down her bag, slipping off her light beige jacket as she did. "Oh, am I the first to arrive?"

Before she could answer, Bev walked in, her chestnut brown hair swept back into a no-nonsense bun.

"Evening, both."

Bev was the former sheriff of Thistle Grove. Lean, strong, and in her sixties, she was often blunt and-to-the point, with piercing blue eyes that could still make you feel as if you were under interrogation. She'd once told Maisie she'd taken up knitting during the long, slow hours between calls at the department, and now she enjoyed making baby beanies for the neonatal ward at the local hospital.

"You should have worn your jacket," Cherry said, shuffling in after Bev with her eleven-year-old daughter, Eloise. "Hi everybody."

"Whatever, I'm fine," the girl muttered, rolling her eyes. While Cherry had the hood of her light spring jacket up,

Eloise wore only a T-shirt and leggings, her cheeks bright pink from the cool evening breeze and her dark curls fluffed by the wind. She made a beeline for the rocking chair in the corner, already shrugging off her backpack.

"*Whatever?*" Ree raised her eyebrows at Cherry. "How old is she now? Eleven going on sixteen?"

"Honestly, some days it feels like it," Cherry laughed. She pulled down her hood and ran a hand through her fiery-red bob. The color not only matched her name, but it was also her hallmark on the roller derby circuit, where she went by "Cherry Contrary."

Maisie hadn't been sure about Cherry when she'd first met her. Tough-looking with a half-sleeve of tattoos running up both arms and multiple piercings in both ears, she came across as edgy and feisty. But Cherry was a single mum, and while she might look tough, the cute crochet animals she made every week said far more about her quirky, caring nature.

Once they'd gotten to know each other, Cherry had confided that her ex—Eloise's dad—was unreliable and mostly out of the picture. Consequently, Cherry was raising her daughter single-handedly, and was doing a wonderful job of it, in Maisie's opinion.

"After you," boomed a loud voice as a large hand held open the door for the next two arrivals.

In bounced MJ, a lively twenty-something who'd dropped out of business school and was taking a year off to figure out what she wanted to do next. She looked bright and breezy in a fire-engine red jacket and a thrifted gold beret perched at a jaunty angle over her long black hair.

Behind her was Brian Featherstone, the only male member of the group. Brian was in his late forties and the local librarian. Although his broad shoulders and thickset build might have made him the ideal defensive tackle in high school, he now was decidedly more interested in history books and rare texts. Married to Brian who owned an auto repair shop in the next town, he spent his free time hiking and knitting sweaters for their pair of sausage dogs, Lucy and Ethel.

"Welcome, everybody." Maisie she set the bread board with the ginger loaf down on the table. "The coffee is fresh and if we're all here, let's get started."

Mewsly wandered over to her basket by the yarn display and began kneading it with both front paws.

MJ bent to pet her. "The cuteness!" She gave Mewsly a few long strokes causing the tabby to purr louder than a sewing machine and stop pawing her blanket.

Bev hung her sensible raincoat over a blue Windsor chair, then joined MJ to give Mewsly a few head scratches. "Every time I feel tempted to stop by the shelter now that Stanley's passed, I remember I can get all the cat cuddles I need from Mewsly."

MJ's eyes widened. "Bev! You didn't tell me you were thinking about adopting a kitten! You *so* should."

"MJ, she's trying *not* to adopt a kitten," Ree laughed from her position at the coffee maker. "I'm with you, Bev. Having a fur baby in the house is a lot of work."

"Mewsly is very easy going," Maisie cut in. Then she pursed her lips. "She is a tripping hazard though."

Bev chuckled and straightened up. "That's true. It's tempting though."

"Don't listen to them," MJ whispered, leaning closer to Bev. "My friend fosters kittens for the shelter. There's this adorable little calico you would *love*."

"Does anyone else want coffee? I'm pouring," Ree called.

"There's half-caf and regular-strength hazelnut," added Maisie.

"Half-caf for me." Bev made her way over to the machine. "Flavored coffee's never been my thing."

"You don't even take cream," Cherry remarked, unloading her crochet supplies. "People who drink black coffee are a different breed."

Bev chuckled. "Maybe so. I like my coffee like I like my witness statements. No frills and straight to the point."

"You can take a girl out of the sheriff's department..." Maisie chortled. "Now where did I leave my mug?"

"Over here." MJ retrieved it from a cubbyhole of yarn. It was a handmade clay mug with Thistle Grove in a pale-pink flowery font written along the middle. "Ooh, I like this. You always have the cutest mugs."

"That was my very first find at the local farmers market," Maisie said with a grin.

"Is anyone else coming?" Cherry asked, one eye on her daughter as Eloise stacked her hot chocolate with marsh-mallows.

"Margot might stop by," Maisie said.

Brian's eyebrows tilted in surprise. "Margot? I haven't seen her in a while."

"Neither have I." Ree arched a brow. "I wonder where she's been hiding."

"Just busy, as far as I know," Maisie said. She'd seen her at the general supply store earlier that day. "She's been working long hours on that tapestry for the town's anniversary."

Margot Bellamy was a local textile artist and frequent member of the Friday evening circle. A few months ago, she had been commissioned by the mayor, Greg Penrose, to create a richly detailed tapestry to celebrate Thistle Grove's

150-year anniversary. A project understandably too large and unwieldy to lug into the store for Knit and Natter nights.

"That's great," Cherry said with a pleased nod. "It'll be good to see her, and I'm dying to find out how it's coming on."

"Tapestries are fascinating," Brian added, his eyes shining. "Traditionally, they're filled with symbolism and important historical details. Take the Bayeux Tapestry for example. It depicts the events leading up to the Norman conquest of England and the Battle of Hastings in 1066."

"Really?" Eloise asked, glancing up.

"Yes, it's kept in a museum in Bayeux, France, hence the name. You should go and see it sometime, if you ever get the chance." His eyes gleamed. "It's quite something."

Eloise looked at her mom, who nodded. "One day, right kiddo?"

The teenager nodded eagerly.

Right on cue, the bell above the door jangled and Margot blustered in, a bag draped over her shoulder and a tray of brownies balanced on one arm.

"Let me help you." Cherry hopped up and took the tray from her.

"Thanks," said Margot with a grateful smile. A tall, middle-aged woman with a blunt cut bob of dark hair streaked with silver, she had a distinctive fashion style and was seldom seen without a pair of oversized glasses. Today's pair had emerald-green frames.

She buttoned her jacket and walked around the table to the empty seat beside Maisie. "It's nice to be here. I didn't think I was going to make it."

"Glad you could join us," Maisie said. "Coffee?"

"None for me, thanks." Margot sank into the chair, and

for a brief moment, Maisie thought she saw her arms shake as she lowered herself to the seat.

"How's the tapestry?" she asked, thinking Margot looked tired. "You managing all right?"

Something flickered in Margot's eyes, but it was quickly replaced by a smile. "I'm nearly done, but I'd be lying if I said it wasn't hard work."

"I can't wait to see the finished item," Brian enthused. "I was just saying how much historical detail goes into the works. Have you put much of Thistle Grove into it?"

"Maybe too much," she said, with a wry grimace, and then unpacked her knitting needles and yarn. Maisie frowned. Margot was unusually subdued and unanimated, which wasn't like her.

"What are you making, Cherry?" Bev pointed to the lizard-like shape Cherry was crocheting.

"It's a salamander," Brian decided, tilting his head.

"Actually, it's an axolotl," Eloise piped up from the rocking chair, clutching her mug. "She's making it for my birthday."

"Aren't birthday presents supposed to be surprises?" Bev asked.

Cherry snorted. "Not this time. El started asking me to make this for her before her last birthday party was even over. I just had to get *really* good at crochet animals first."

As the group continued chatting, Maisie got up to fetch her own knitting project from the back room, having completely forgotten to bring it out. When she reached the kitchenette, she realized Margot had followed her.

"I'd like a glass of water, if that's all right?" Margot nodded towards the sink.

"Of course." Maisie grabbed an empty glass from the cupboard and filled it from the tap.

She handed it to Margot, who took a long drink.

"You okay?" Maisie asked.

"It's just been a long week," she said, setting the glass down on the countertop.

"It would be with a project like that. What is it, a few *hundred* strands?" Maisie asked, retrieving her knitting.

"Try fifteen threads per inch," Margot retorted. "For an eighty-inch tapestry, that's more like a thousand just for the warp."

"The warp threads are the vertical ones, right?" Maisie wrinkled her forehead, trying to remember. "That must make the welt the horizontal threads."

Margot nodded. "That's right."

Maisie turned to go back to the table, when Margot grabbed her arm. "Maisie—" She bit her lip.

"Yes?" Margot's grip was tight. "What is it? Are you sure you're all right?"

Margot took a shuddering breath. "Maisie, if anything happens to me...will you finish the tapestry?"

"What do you mean?" Maisie frowned, alarmed. "Nothing's going to happen to you."

"I know, but if it does," Margot insisted, her fingers digging into Maisie's forearm, "promise me you'll finish it?"

Maisie shook her head. What she knew about tapestry making wouldn't fill a thimble, but she saw the fear behind the red-framed glasses. "Margot, what is this about? Are you ill? Has something happened?"

"No, nothing like that."

"But—?"

"There's not much left to do," she went on. "And what you don't know, you can learn."

"Margot—?"

"You have to promise, Maisie. There are things in it only you can see."

"Thinks? What things? Margot, you're not making any sense."

"Please—" Her look was pleading.

Maisie sighed. "Yes, of course. But if there's something wrong, maybe I can help?"

"You are helping by agreeing to do this." On that cryptic note, Margot went to rejoin the others at the table.

After a few seconds, Maisie did the same.

Chapter 2

Not A Good Morning

The next morning, Maisie awoke to a late-night text from Margot. It had come in at 2 a.m., while Maisie's phone was on silent.

Forgot my journal at the store last night. Hold onto it for me?

Maisie squinted at the bright light of her phone screen. She hadn't even seen Margot with a journal the night before. Her friend's strange demeanor and her mysterious request replayed in her mind.

If anything happens to me, promise me you'll finish the tapestry.

For a moment, she pondered whether she should text back with more questions, to get to the bottom of what Margot had said.

No. Better to talk to her in person.

As it happened, Margot had ordered some custom, hand-dyed wool a few days before but had forgotten to collect it last night. Maisie sent a reply.

No problem! I've got your wool order. OK if I stop by?

"Morning, Mews." Maisie sat up in bed and reached over to pet Mewsly, who was curled up at her feet. "You going to join me at the shop today?"

Mewsly didn't deign to reply and kept her eyes closed.

"Okay, fine. Stay here then, you lazy thing."

Maisie stroked her for a few more moments, then left her to snooze.

After straightening the bed and pulling open the curtains to a soft, silvery spring sky, she made her way to the kitchen for a cup of coffee.

The house she shared with Mewsly was small but cozy. It was really more cottage than house, with white weatherboard siding, a peaked roof, and navy-blue shutters. It had once belonged to an elderly woman who hadn't changed much over the years, leaving behind a quiet, lived-in charm that Maisie appreciated. The place reminded her of the homes in old Doris Day films, where everything felt tidy, warm, and just a little worn in around the edges.

Maisie had renovated it right away, thanks to Frankie's life insurance payout—a bittersweet gift that had helped her begin this new chapter. She and Mewsly had lived out of one of the home's two bedrooms while contractors refreshed the bathroom and kitchen and opened up the narrow hallway to create a brighter, more welcoming living space.

The end result was exactly what she'd wanted. A sunny, modernized cottage with heaps of character. She filled it with an eclectic mix of comfortable and antique furniture, then brought it to life with potted plants and artwork she and Frankie had collected on their travels. It was the little splashes of color that made the house feel hopeful again, she thought to herself, as she switched on the coffee maker.

"Ah, hungry are we?" She chuckled as a sleepy Mewsly appeared in the kitchen, mewing and winding around her ankles.

Maisie fed the now loudly meowing furball breakfast, then checked the time. Weekends were busy at the store. Sew Something at ten o'clock reliably brought in at least a dozen people. If she wanted to stop in and see Margot, she'd have to leave a little earlier.

"Heading out in thirty minutes," she told Mewsly, who had almost finished gobbling her food.

Twenty-nine minutes later, Maisie held the front door for Mewsly to dart through, then locked up. Still no reply from Margot, but she decided to stop by anyway. Draped in a breezy floral scarf and a light denim jacket, her patchwork tote stuffed full of hand-dyed yarn, she headed down the sidewalk toward the center of town.

Margot's home, which doubled as her studio, was conveniently situated on Main Street, only a few doors down from Tangled Threads. Her front door was almost directly across from Dillard's Bakehouse, the bakery next door, famous for its sourdough, cinnamon buns, and a staunch favorite amongst her regulars.

She set a brisk pace, enjoying the mild April morning air, her low-heeled boots tapping on the sun-warmed sidewalk. Mewsly ran ahead down the concrete, her tail held high like a little banner, then disappeared around the corner and out of sight.

"Bye, Mews." One day she'd buy a tiny cat cam, so she could see what Mewsly got up to on her adventures.

Thistle Grove was quiet, which was usual for this early on a Saturday morning. The town center, only a twenty-minute walk away, would be buzzing with shoppers, brunch-goers and wine-lovers by ten-thirty.

Nestled in the Willamette Valley, the lush green hills around Thistle Grove, were thick with forests and vineyards. The region boasted some world-renown wineries, but she'd yet to explore them. They did bring in the tourists, though, and now spring was approaching, the tasting rooms and restaurants were doing a thriving trade.

Oregon springs were cooler than what Maisie had grown used to in LA, but after almost a year back in her home state, she'd happily built a new wardrobe of light sweaters, soft scarves, and comfortable boots—layers she could peel off as the day warmed.

She'd always loved fashion, right from a young age. Barbies were her first guinea pigs, followed by a series of outfits fashioned for the long-suffering family pooch. After falling in love with drama in high school, she'd gone on to study costume design in university, cutting her teeth on the local theatre scene.

A few years after graduation, adventure in the big city had called. Maisie sucked in a deep lungful of fresh air and let it out again. Life in LA had been fast-paced and fun. Every new film project she worked on felt like she was helping to create a whole new world.

And, of course, there had been Frankie.

Darling Frank.

She remembered the day they'd met like it was yesterday. He'd bumped into her on a film set, literally, and the armful of costumes she'd been carrying had tumbled to the floor. He'd apologized and bent to help her pick them up. Their eyes had locked over a Victorian bodice, and the rest, as they say, was history.

Frank had worked his way up in the industry as a cameraman, so he understood both her passion for her art and the long hours demanded by life on set. They'd had long, passionate discussions about drama, film and the theatre. They saw plays on Broadway, travelled to London, Paris and Rome, always on location, always working, but it was doing something they both loved. And they had each other.

Maisie glanced down at her wedding ring, sparkling in the morning sunlight. It was an antique piece that had first belonged to Frankie's grandmother and she loved the circle of tiny, old-cut diamonds surrounding a rich ruby set in warm yellow gold.

It had been a fine spring day, not unlike this one, when he'd proposed. It had been five years into their relationship, when Frank had pulled the ring box out of his pocket and got down on one knee.

Forever? had been the easiest question Maisie had ever said yes to.

A young mother pushing a stroller on the opposite side of the street waved at her. Maisie smiled and waved back. The woman had come in on a Saturday morning a few weeks ago and Maisie had been more than happy to hold the baby while she learned the basics on the sewing machine.

Having children had always been an idea floating on the horizon for her and Frankie, but nothing had ever fallen into place. Life in the film industry was feast or famine. Either one or both of them were often away from home on location or putting in eighteen-hour days on set, or weeks would pass between jobs.

Neither had minded very much. Mewsly was their baby and well cared for by a loyal lineup of cat sitters. The years ahead had seemed so limitless—until one drunk driver had changed everything.

Still, that was in the past now, and this cute town—Thistle Grove—was her future. She didn't regret packing up her LA condo and coming back to the valley, the place where she'd grown up. It felt like coming home.

There was nothing left for her in L.A. anyway, and here, she had space to grow, but time to heal.

Maisie turned up Grover Street, passing ranch and Cape Cod–style houses with generous front yards. Margot's two-story brick and weatherboard house was on the corner with Main.

She'd been there a few times, thanks to the warm welcome Margot had given her when she first arrived in town. The tapestry maker had been one of the first people to drop by Tangled Threads when the doors had opened, and she'd wasted no time in inviting Maisie to lunch. Through Margot, she had met several other locals, including some of the now-regulars at her Knit and Natter nights.

Maisie reached into her pocket and checked her phone. Still no reply. Frowning, she sent another message.

Hey, did you get my last text?

She was almost at the corner of Grover and Main now. Gnawing on her lower lip, Maisie dashed off a follow-up.

Might stop by anyway. See you soon.

As she approached the corner, sounds of the town center carried over the air. She heard car doors slamming, the rumble of engines, and faint music from a nearby diner as the door was pushed open and swung shut again.

Margot's house, white but with a red front door, looked unassumingly quiet. Only one fluffy white dog in the window of the house next door noted Maisie's presence with furious barking as she passed and made her way up the front steps.

She knocked, but there was no answer.

She tried again, then leaned over to look through one of the two long windows that framed the door. To her surprise, she saw her own cat inside.

"Mewsly? What on earth are you doing there?" Maisie exclaimed.

She tapped on the glass until Mewsly looked up at her. The cat meowed, the sound trapped behind the double panes.

Where was Margot?

Hesitantly, Maisie tried the door. To her surprise, it was unlocked. That was strange. Margot never left the front door open.

"Hello?" she called, opening it and sticking her head inside. "Margot? Margot, it's Maisie, I'm coming in."

She took a few steps into the foyer and frowned at Mewsly. "How did you get in here?"

Mewsly stared at her with round, unblinking eyes, then turned tail and ran deeper into the house. Clucking with annoyance, Maisie followed.

"I'm so sorry," she called loudly. "Mewsly got in here somehow. Margot?"

She turned the corner into the living room. Margot's tall, free-standing tapestry loom stood there, strung with dozens of horizontal and vertical threads that framed an exquisite, nearly completed tapestry.

"Wow!" Maisie stepped closer and admired the tightly woven fabric.

Normally, Margot worked out of a studio at the back of the house, but this piece was clearly too large to fit.

Maisie studied it, almost reverently. Most of the design

was finished, with only the last few inches at the top left to complete. The piece was reminiscent of a medieval tapestry, woven from vibrant, earthy shades of gold, cream, brown, deep red, and green. A rich brown border framed the scene, highlighted in places with distinctive wavy lines. The town crest sat at the bottom middle.

It was stunning.

She noticed several notable landmarks. There was Penrose House, a stately home that served as the town hall. The local church, it's spire stretching into the sky. A few historic shop fronts, and in the background, rows of grapevines and stands of trees.

Flora and fauna encroached onto the scene from either side, and in what she assumed was the town green, there was a burst of flames that no doubt represented Thistle Grove's annual autumn bonfire.

Margot had outdone herself.

Where was she?

Maisie walked back into the hallway. "Margot? I love what you've done so far. It's incredible."

Mewsly meowed from somewhere down the hall. What was that cat up to now? Probably in the kitchen, looking for scraps.

Maisie marched after her, but the kitchen was vacant. Glancing up, she caught sight of Margot's studio at the back of the house.

That's where she must be.

Mewsly stood at the entrance, her tail stiff.

Pushing open the door, Maisie stepped into the studio— then froze.

Margot lay motionless on her back just inside the studio door, her skin mottled and her pajamas soaked with blood.

"Margot!" Maisie dropped to her knees to help her, but

she was too late. Her friend wasn't breathing. It was then she spotted the gold handle of a small pair of scissors sticking out from the other side of her neck.

Maisie choked back a sob.

Please, no.

Heart hammering, she fumbled for her phone.

With trembling fingers, she dialed 911.

Chapter 3

Knit and Natter

Sheriff Markham and Deputy Andy Summers arrived within ten minutes. Maisie met them outside the house by the red front door, where she had gone to wait rather than linger near Margot's body.

She still couldn't believe she was dead. Who—? Why—? The questions spun around and around in her head, and she felt like it was filled with cottonwool. It wasn't dissimilar to how she'd felt when she'd heard Frank had died.

Shock. She knew the signs well.

Markham, elected sheriff after Bev had retired, was in his late forties, heavyset with a grumpy, but ultimately fair demeanor that rubbed more than a few people the wrong way.

"Like a school principal with a hockey stick up his butt," Bev had once described him. Looking at him now, a deep crevice between his eyes and his mouth turned down at the edges, Maisie thought it rather apt.

Deputy Andy, by contrast, was tall, gangly, and cheery, most of the time. The rookie of the department, he was somewhere in his late twenties but only a year out of the Academy.

While Markham eased himself out of the patrol car like an old cowboy dismounting a horse, Andy sprang out like a frisky cricket.

"Hi, Maisie," Andy said. He wasn't smiling now. She knew him from around town, but not personally. Thankfully, their paths had never crossed. Until now.

"She's inside," Maisie muttered, clutching Mewsly to her chest. For once, Mewsly was still, but she watched the deputy with suspicious eyes.

He gave a tight nod. "Stay here. We'll go check it out."

Hand poised on the holster of his service weapon, he disappeared inside.

"Ms. Button," nodded Sheriff Markham as he strode past. "We'll need to ask you a few questions. Don't go anywhere."

"I won't."

Mewsly wriggled frantically, so Maisie set her down on the ground. The tabby, having had enough of the crime scene, darted off behind a hedge.

Maisie watched her go, willing her heart to stop racing. Now the initial shock was wearing off, she felt shaky and tired. Walking over to a low wall, she sat down.

If anything happens to me, complete the tapestry.

Maisie gasped as Margot's words came back to her.

She wrapped her arms around herself as she thought about what that meant. Margot must have known she was in danger. And now she was dead.

Maisie was still deep in thought when Sheriff Markham reappeared.

"Could you join us inside," he asked, although it was in a tone that meant she didn't dare refuse.

She didn't want to venture back into the house, but steeling her shoulders, she did as he asked. Thankfully, he led her into the living room and motioned for her to sit down.

She sank into an armchair. Margot's armchair. A lump caught in her throat.

"I believe you discovered the body?" he began.

She nodded. "Yes, I came to visit Margot. I wanted to drop off some wool." She stared down at her tote bag, still hanging over her shoulder. Shrugging it off, she placed it on the floor at her feet. The colorful skeins of soft new yarn Margot had ordered were visible through the open top. Her chest tightened. "But when I knocked, there was no answer. I called for Margot, but I didn't hear anything."

"How did you get in?" Sheriff Markham asked, a bushy eyebrow nudging upward.

"The door was unlocked."

He studied her. "Are you in a habit of entering people's homes when they're not there?"

"Mewsly was inside."

"Muesli?" He cocked his head to the side.

"My cat," she clarified, before he thought she'd broken in looking for breakfast cereal. "I saw her through the glass panel in the door."

He stared at her, confused.

Maisie drew in a breath. She wasn't making any sense. "She likes to visit people, and I guess she found a way in."

"That the brown tabby?" Deputy Andy asked, coming

into the living room. "She came and saw us at the department the other day. Friendly little thing."

Sheriff Markham snorted, clearly not a cat person. "Okay, so you saw your cat, then you came in?"

"Yes. I tried the door and it was unlocked, so I poked my head in to call for Margot. When she didn't answer, I got worried and went looking for her. It's not like her to leave her front door unlocked. She's normally pretty security conscious."

Sheriff Markham nodded at Deputy Andy. "Check all the doors and windows for a possible point of entry."

Deputy Andy looked surprised. "For the cat?"

"No, for the *perpetrator*," the sheriff barked. "And check to see if any obvious items of high value are missing."

As the deputy hurried off on his mission, Markham turned back to Maisie. "Please, go on."

"Like I said, I called Margot, but there was no answer. I thought she might be in her studio, which is out back." She stopped as the image of Margot lying on the floor crashed through her mind.

Clearing her throat, she finished, "That's when I saw her... and called you."

"You make contact with the body? Move anything, touch anything?"

Maisie masked a little gasp. "I may have touched her. I knelt down to see if she was okay. That's when I realized..." She paused. "I realized she wasn't breathing. Then I called you."

Markham considered this for a moment. "You didn't see anyone else in the house? Hear anybody leave?"

"No. It was just me—and Mewsly."

He frowned at the cat's name, but gave a gruff nod.

"Maisie?" a voice called from the front door. "What's going on?"

Sheriff Markham got to his feet just as MJ appeared in the living room entrance.

"Why is the sheriff here? Where's Margot?"

Before Sheriff Markham could say anything, Deputy Andy appeared in the doorway.

"I'm sorry, ma'am, but this is an active crime scene. You're not permitted to be here. This is an active crime scene."

MJ put her hands on her hips. "Don't you ma'am me, Andy."

He froze, his ruddy cheeks turning pink. "Oh. Hi, MJ."

The sheriff shook his head. "Deputy, please escort these ladies outside."

"What do you mean, a crime scene?" MJ asked, glancing from Andy to Maisie, and then to the sheriff.

Maisie got up and went to MJ, taking both of her hands. "It's Margot," she said gently. "She's been killed."

MJ gasped. "What do you mean, 'killed'? Margot was *murdered*?"

"We don't know that for certain," Sheriff Markham said loudly, shooting Andy a look of intense irritation. "It could have been an accident."

"An accident?" Maisie turned to face him. "She was stabbed with a pair of embroidery scissors."

MJ gasped again. "Margot was *stabbed*?"

Markham looked like he was about to implode. Andy hastily escorted them out.

The sheriff followed. "Deputy, what did you find?"

"The back door was open," Andy reported over his shoulder. "A few drawers were dumped out upstairs in the bedroom."

"Could be a break-in gone wrong. The burglar gained access to the property, Ms. Bellamy surprised him, and he killed her with whatever weapon was available."

Maisie couldn't help herself. "Surely a burglar is more likely to run away than commit murder?"

Sheriff Markham levelled her with a stern look. "I didn't realize you were an expert, Ms. Button."

"Oh, I'm not. Murder just doesn't seem like a very burglary thing to do."

Markham actually rolled his eyes.

Beside her, MJ was tearing up. "I can't believe this. How can she be dead? We only saw her yesterday."

"Yesterday?" Andy asked.

Maisie nodded. "Yes, she came into the store. She's part of our Friday evening Knit and Natter group."

"Your what?" Markham asked, scowling.

Maisie looked at Andy. "She was acting a bit strangely."

He frowned. "How so?"

"I don't know. She was saying weird things, and she also left her journal behind."

"Why is that strange?" Markham asked.

"She's never usually forgetful," MJ cut in with a sniff.

Maisie put an arm around her friend's shoulders. "You'll find out who did this?" she asked, still looking at Andy.

He gave a stiff nod. "We'll do our very best, Maisie."

"We'll be in touch if we need anything," Markham said, effectively dismissing them.

"Wait. The tapestry!" Maisie said, halting suddenly. Andy, who was following them nearly bumped into her back.

"What?" he asked.

"She was working on a tapestry for the town's anniversary. Can we at least take a picture of it?"

Markham appeared in the doorway. "You'd better show me this tapestry."

Maisie turned back into the house. "It's in the studio."

"Let's go," Markham said, gesturing for her to lead the way.

Gulping, Maisie retraced her footsteps from earlier, through the kitchen and into the studio. She avoided looking at Margot's prone body, still lying in the doorway.

MJ spotted it and gasped, then turned away. Andy was there and put an arm around her. She buried her face in his chest. "Oh, my gosh. It's so awful."

"Don't look," he said, leading her back into the kitchen.

"I'll get it," Markham said, and straining, he lifted it up and carried it out into the kitchen, careful to step around Margot's body.

"Are you sure about that, Sheriff? It might be evidence," Andy said. MJ was sitting at the kitchen table, her head in her hands.

"This is a half-finished art project, Summers. It wasn't valuable enough to steal, and it was nowhere near the body."

"But—"

"You can take it," he said to Maisie. "If you can carry it, that is."

"We can carry it," MJ said, wiping tears from her cheeks.

Andy glanced at the sheriff, then back at MJ. "Let me give you a hand."

The sheriff made to protest, but Andy added, "I'll be right back."

With an exasperated sigh, Markham let them go.

It was six o'clock and Maisie was exhausted. It had been a busy day at Tangled Threads, which was probably a good thing considering what had happened this morning.

Word had spread, and almost the entire Knit and Natter circle had come to offer their commiserations—and to discuss the murder.

"I can't believe she's dead," Ree whispered, her lined face pale.

"With her own scissors," Cherry added, with a shudder.

"Who'd want to kill Margot?" Brian said, shaking his head.

They all gathered around the farmhouse table staring at the tapestry.

About the weight of a large mirror, it hadn't been easy to carry, so Andy had taken pity on them and transported it here in his cruiser.

The last of the day's sunlight had faded into a dreary dusk, and clouds had moved in, making it appear darker than usual.

Mewsly was curled up in her basket by the yarn display, and as everyone gazed at Margot's work, the only sounds were purring and the full-bodied spluttering of the coffee maker.

"I can't stop thinking about what Margot said," Brian murmured, breaking the silence. "That if anything happened to her, to finish the tapestry."

"She must have known," Bev said.

Ree shook her head. "I wish she'd confided in us."

Cherry reached out and gently touched the edge of the tapestry. "It's very beautiful. Such intricate details."

Eloise stood beside her, inspecting the design with the others.

"I can't believe the sheriff let you take this," Ree said. "I would have thought it was evidence, considering what Margot asked you to do."

"I didn't exactly share with him what she said."

They all turned to stare at her.

"Why not?" Bev asked, eyes slanting.

"It wouldn't have made any difference," MJ cut in. Markham's convinced it was a bungled burglary."

Maisie nodded. "It was pretty obvious he didn't want us there."

"I always knew he was an idiot," muttered Bev.

"Is that the Thistle Grove sawmill?" Brian asked, leaning in for a closer look.

Maisie nodded. She'd studied it in detail that afternoon. "That's the town green, Penrose House, and what I think is Main Street."

Eloise nodded. "It looks like it. Not this bit, though."

"What did Margot mean that there are things in the tapestry that only you can see?" Cherry asked, frowning. "Do you think she meant she'd left clues in the tapestry?"

"Like a hidden message?" Eloise said, face lighting up.

"Maybe," Cherry agreed, ruffling her daughter's hair.

"I don't know," Maisie mused. She'd had the same thought but dismissed it as a fancy. "All this looks pretty normal to me."

"The symbols might not be hidden, *per se*," Brian said, turning to face them. "Historically speaking, tapestries tell stories though the images chosen by the weaver. A figure touching their face, for example, could be a sign of grief or mourning. A unicorn often meant purity."

"A unicorn?" Ree frowned. "I think you've had too much coffee, Brian."

"What about the flowers?" MJ pointed to a cluster of blossoms in the foreground. "The Victorians attributed all kinds of meanings to them. Violets for happiness, marigolds for jealousy—that sort of thing."

"Could be," Brian agreed. "Also, we should look at the places and items Margot chose to include. They might have a specific meaning."

"It's all town landmarks, from what I can see," said Bev, squinting at it. "I wish we knew what we were looking for."

Behind them, the coffee maker sputtered to a finish.

MJ clicked her fingers, then dug into her pocket for her phone. "Actually, Margot sent me the original design for the tapestry. This was before she started it. She wanted my feedback."

"Can we see it?" Brian asked.

She held up her phone. "Here it is. It's pretty detailed, you can't make out much from this image."

"Maybe we can print it out and enlarge it?" Cherry suggested.

"My printer's out of ink," Maisie said, ruefully.

"Just send it to each other," Eloise piped up, rolling her eyes. "Or airdrop it."

"Air-what it?" Ree asked, blinking at her.

"You know, using Bluetooth."

Cherry stared at her daughter. "How d'you know about that? You don't even have a phone."

Maisie knew Cherry had been holding off, but the time was coming when she'd have to get her one. It was to be a twelfth birthday present.

Eloise shrugged. "Everybody knows that."

Ree met Maisie's gaze with a raised eyebrow. "Not everyone, dear."

After rummaging through bags and coat pockets, everyone pulled out their phones. MJ sent through the image of the sketch. For a few minutes, there was a hushed quiet as the group studied the picture. Slowly, each member began glancing up at Margot's tapestry.

"There!" Cherry pointed to the top part. "The cross on the church is upside down. What does that mean? Could it be some kind of religious corruption?"

"The bonfire," Ree added, leaning in. "At first, I thought it was our town's annual Labor Day festivities, but there's something small in the flames. A person, I think."

Maisie peered in. There was indeed a figure in the flames. The hairs on her neck bristled. It was so small she'd completely missed it.

"The borders are different too," pointed out Brian, adjusting his readers. "In Margot's sketch, there weren't any squiggly marks."

Maisie stared at the tapestry. "Incredible. Once you compare the two designs, you can spot the differences."

"It is just like a puzzle," Eloise said.

"I wonder what it means?" MJ glanced around the group.

Brian stroked his chin. "There are a few resources I could look at, but I've never seen any symbolism in tapestry that looks like this."

"That's because Margot was sending *us* a message," MJ said. "Or rather, Maisie. The tapestry is how she's sending it, but the message is for us. We're the only ones who can figure it out." Her eyes took on a determined glint. "I say we conduct our own investigation."

Maisie hesitated. "What about the sheriff? Shouldn't we tell him about this?"

Ree scoffed. "You said yourself that Sheriff Markham isn't taking an interest."

"That's right. He told us we could take it," MJ cut in.

"I agree." Cherry gave a firm nod. "We need answers. Margot deserves answers."

Bev pursed her lips. It was no secret that she wasn't a fan of Sheriff Markham. "Couldn't hurt to do a little investigating."

Maisie looked at the determined and concerned expressions on her friends' faces. They wanted to do this, she thought. For Margot. Deep down, so did she.

Margot had asked—no, begged—her to complete the tapestry. She'd told Maisie there was something important hidden there for her to find, and it was obvious she'd made changes to the original design. If the sheriff wasn't going to take the tapestry seriously, the least she could do was to honor Margot's last request and look into the clues her friend had left behind.

"Okay," she breathed. "Let's do it."

There was a general murmur of approval. Eloise clapped her hands, startling a dosing Mewsly who jumped off her lap. "I love riddles."

"How do you want to proceed?" Cherry asked.

Maisie thought for a moment. "Everyone take a photograph of the actual tapestry, and we can start coming up with theories on what Margot was trying to tell us. We'll meet back here every few days to compare notes."

"Every day," MJ decided. "We should meet every day until we figure this out. It's important."

Those were Margot's words too.

It's important.

There was a nod of consensus amongst the group.

"Okay, fine," Maisie agreed. "How about we meet here at six every evening after closing? If we work together, we may be able to help the sheriff solve this mystery—and find Margot's killer."

"I'm all for that," Cherry said. Eloise gave an excited yelp.

"Agreed," added Brian.

"Count me in," said Ree.

Even Bev gave a nod.

That was a resounding yes, then.

Chapter 4

A Tragic Tale

After opening up the next morning, Maisie stood at the front window, sipping a strong coffee and staring out at the pale sky. The leaves on the trees dotted along Main Street were beginning to flesh out, ridding them of that stark winter look. There were even some birds chirping in them.

Conversely, she hadn't woken up in the best of moods. Margot's death sat heavily on her, and she couldn't stop seeing her friends face, the knife sticking out of her neck. To cheer herself up, she'd worn her favorite, red-knit sweater over a soft, cream blouse, and added a cluster of silver bangles that tinkled when she moved.

The store had been open for half an hour already, but Maisie had only welcomed one customer so far. The slow start was needed, after the night of tossing and turning she'd had. Margot, the tapestry, and the discrepancies she and the Knit and Natter group had found had plagued her dreams.

What did it all mean? The church with its upside-down cross. The small figure in the flames. Squiggles in the borders.

When she'd woken up this morning, the only thing she was sure about was that whatever Margot had been trying to say, it must have something to do with the town's history.

But what? And why would someone want to kill her over it?

Maisie sighed. A year in Thistle Grove did not make her an expert on the town's past, let alone any secrets hidden in the tapestry.

From her basket by the yarn display, Mewsly stretched, yawned, and curled back up again. Maisie wandered over to give her cat a few long strokes.

"I wish I could curl up in there with you," she mused, running her palm along the cat's black-ribbed fur. Mewsly's little motor came to life and she purred contentedly. "But that's not going to help solve this puzzle, is it, Mews?"

As soon as she said it, an idea came to her. Back when she'd worked as a costume designer, every new project had begun the same way. Before a single sketch, before a single fabric choice, there was research. Weeks of it. She always started by learning everything she could about the world her characters lived in. How they dressed, how they moved through their days, and what details made their lives feel real.

"That's how I'll start," she decided, straightening up. "If I'm going to figure out what this tapestry is telling us, I have to know more about everything on it. Right, Mews?"

Mewsly rolled over in her basket, exposing her belly. Maisie snorted. "After belly rubs, of course."

A few minutes later, a customer came in, and gradually the store got busier. For the first time since it had happened, Maisie was forced to think of something other than Margot's death or the tapestry.

She spent the better part of the day helping customers find patterns, choose fabrics, and decide on weights of yarn. She pointed an eight-year-old bunny enthusiast to a craft kit for making felt animals and helped a grandmother dig through the rummage drawer of loose buttons for a replacement for a child's dress she was updating.

Midafternoon, there was a lull in foot traffic. Taking advantage, Maisie threw open the front door and stepped out of the shop for some fresh air. It felt good after having been inside all day. Mewsly had already left the premises, having bolted out between a customer's feet sometime around noon.

She hung a cross-stitched *Out for Lunch* sign on the door and locked up. Then, glancing up and down the street, she set off for her favorite sandwich shop to grab a bite to eat.

It was a lovely afternoon. The pale blue sky bathed the street in warm, yellow sunlight, and the spring air was fresh with the scent of blossoms. By the time she got there, she was starving. It hadn't been a good idea to skip lunch, but she'd been so busy, the thought hadn't crossed her mind.

She was about to push open the door when she spotted a community notice board in the window. Stopping, she stepped to the side to read it. Most of the faded notices were out of date. The store owner should really update them. Then, an advertisement for an event that had taken place the previous March, caught her eye.

*Learn about the fascinating history of Thistle Grove with
local historian Drew Buckland. Thistle Grove Historical
Society. Tea, coffee, and cookies included.*

Below, it gave the address.

"Local historian," Maisie muttered as she went into the
shop. That was exactly who she needed to talk to.

BLT in hand, Maisie went in search of the historical
society. Conscious of the time, she set at a brisk pace. She
couldn't leave the store unattended for too long.

When she got to the address, she discovered the historical society operated not from a brick building or shopfront,
but from a white weatherboard colonial-style home with a
wide grey roof, pale blue window shutters.

She stared up at the arched doorway at the top of red-
brick front steps. This was someone's home.

Sunk into the green grass of the front lawn was an
ornate wooden sign that read, *Thistle Grove Historical Society, est. 1957.* No opening hours were visible.

As she gazed up at the house, Maisie saw a man in a
collared shirt pass by one of the front windows. A home
converted into an office.

Checking her watch, she decided she could spare a few
minutes.

The same man answered the door within a few seconds
of her knock. Middle-aged, with salt-and-pepper hair and a
soft chin, he seemed delighted to have a visitor.

"Welcome!" He clapped his hands together. "How may
I help you?"

"Are you Drew Buckland?" she asked, remembering the
name on the flyer.

"I am indeed. Who might you be?" He peered over his glasses at her.

"I'm Maisie Button. I own Tangle Threads, the craft store on Main Street."

"Oh, yes. You're fairly new to Thistle Grove. Welcome. Welcome."

She smiled as he beckoned her inside.

"Thank you." She glanced up at the art on the walls. He had an impressive collection of oil and watercolors, along with a few sepia-toned photographs.

"Actually, I'm interested in the town's history. I was hoping you could help me."

"Of course. That's what I'm here for. Please, take a seat." He gestured to a comfy chair opposite a large, mahogany desk in the center of the room, but her gaze flew to a high-backed occasional chair and accompanying foot-stool positioned in the far corner.

"That is a lovely chair," she said, heading over to it instead. She fingered the moss-green brocade upholstery with a raised paisley design.

He let out a surprised, but pleased snort. "That came with the house. I think it's from the twenties or thirties."

"Someone had good taste," she murmured, then laughed, embarrassed. "I used to be a costume designer, so I have a thing for textiles."

"I see. I'm the historian in residence, so this house is both my home and the office of the historical society."

She took a seat where he'd first suggested. "It's lovely."

"Thank you." He sat opposite her and crossed his legs. "What inspired your interest in the history of our town?"

"Margot Bellamy, the textile artist." She took a deep breath, then let it out in a rush. "She was murdered yester-day. I don't know if you heard?"

"Yes. Yes, I did," Buckland bowed his head solemnly. "Terrible news, just tragic. I knew Margot. She came to talk to me about the area's history for the anniversary tapestry she was creating."

That gave Maisie the perfect in.

"I've been asked to complete the tapestry," she told him, her voice faltering just a little. She swallowed over the lump in her throat. "I was hoping to find out what inspired her design. In particular, the landmarks she included. I'm afraid I don't know a lot about the history of Thistle Grove since, as you pointed out, I only recently moved here."

Buckland broke into a smile. "Sure, I can help with that. As with any town, there are a lot of stories in our past, but I'll start with the basics."

"Thank you."

He motioned to a pair of sepia-toned family portraits hanging side by side on the wall. Two families, posed in identical ways. The man standing and the woman sitting, surrounded by two and three children, respectively.

"Those are our founding families," Buckland explained proudly. "The Rutherfords and the Penroses. Almost a hundred and fifty years ago now, hence Margot's commission from the mayor."

He pointed to the portrait on the left. "That's Augustus Rutherford with his wife and two children. He owned the land that Thistle Grove was built on, and beyond. Silas Penrose—" his finger swayed to the other photo "—was his business partner. Whereas Rutherford had the land, Penrose contributed the capital to build the town's infrastructure."

"They founded Thistle Grove together?" Maisie asked, studying the portraits. "I'm sure I've heard the name Rutherford before."

Buckland gave a proud nod. "Both families still live in the area. One of Rutherford's descendants, Franklin, owns Rutherford Timber and Land Management with his wife, Harriet."

Of course. Harriet had come into her store a few times. For yarn, if memory served.

"Really nice couple," continued Buckland. "They're in their sixties now, and thankfully just as interested in preserving the town's heritage as I am. There's a wealth of information in their archives about town planning and land use."

Maisie nodded, filing it away. That was good to note.

"No doubt you've met the Penrose family," Buckland was saying.

"The mayor is a descendant?" Maisie guessed.

"That's right. Greg Penrose is the great-grandson of Silas. His parents, June and William, live at the Sycamore Hill estate, just outside of town. They own the golf resort and hotel."

Maisie recalled driving past the place. "I haven't seen the hotel, but the golf course is very beautiful."

"It's an extensive property," Buckland agreed. "The history is a little sad, though. The original owners were steeped in tragedy."

"Who were they?" Maisie asked, wondering if she had the time to get into this now. But her curiosity was piqued. "What happened?"

"I don't know all the details," he began. "I was just a kid when it happened, and there's limited newspaper coverage of the kidnapping."

Maisie sat up straighter. "Kidnapping?"

He gave a grim nod. "The Hollowells—the couple who owned the property before the Penroses—had their baby stolen. The mother, Ada Hollowell, was a bigshot Hollywood actress, and the father a film director. From what I've read, they moved to Thistle Grove to escape the limelight, only to have their infant son abducted."

Maisie was astounded. How had she never heard about this?

"Did they ever find him?"

Buckland shook his head. "No, and that's not even the worst part. A few months later, their home burned to the ground—with Ada inside."

Maisie gasped, her mind immediately flying to the small figure in the flames. Could that be the fire in Margot's tapestry?

Buckland's cellphone beeped from somewhere on the mahogany desk, and he shot her an apologetic look before rifling through the mounds of paperwork to locate it.

"I'm sorry," he said after scanning the message. "I have to cut our conversation short. I'm hosting an event tonight and need to make a call. I don't know much more about the tragedy, anyway, but I'm sure if you ask some of the older folk around town, they'll be happy to tell you about it."

"Thank you, I'll do that." Maisie got to her feet. "I need to get back to my store anyway. I appreciate your time."

"Margot had a notebook," Buckland said suddenly, as she turned to leave. "She brought it with her whenever she came to see me. Made copious notes. That might shed some more light."

A notebook.

In a flash, Maisie remembered the text she had received from her friend yesterday morning.

Forgot my journal at the store last night. Hold onto it for me?

Maisie felt like leaping across the desk and hugging him. She'd look for it as soon as she got back to the store.

"Thank you," she reiterated. "You've been really helpful."

More than he knew.

Chapter 5

The Mannequin's Secret

"Have you checked between the bolts of fabric?" Maisie asked.

Cherry was rummaging through a shelf of fat quarters, Eloise at her side, working in tandem to refold what her mother knocked loose.

"Why would Margot's notebook be in there?" Ree said, brushing a loose strand of hair from her face. She had just finished going through the balls of chunky yarn and was now moving on to the regular skeins. "I thought she left it here by accident. I can't see her accidentally dropping it behind the flannelette."

"I think Margot hid the journal on purpose," Brian decided. "Possibly to safeguard the clues in the tapestry." He reached into the button drawer and wiggled his fingers against the bottom. The assorted collection of flat discs, tiny knobs, and smooth beads shifted around his hand like colorful quicksand.

"What did the text say again?" MJ asked Maisie. She sat at the farmhouse table, petting a very relaxed and stretched-out Mewsly.

Maisie, who'd read the text so many times she knew it by heart, pushed back the sleeves of her cardigan and crouched down in front of the coffee station. "Margot said she'd forgotten her journal at the store and to hold on to it for her. That's all." She reached underneath the small table to check for anything taped to the underside but came up empty-handed.

"She must have hidden it," Bev remarked, picking up a stack of old craft magazines and checking underneath them. "Forgetting her journal here the night before she was murdered? It can't be a coincidence."

"That's so chilling." Cherry shivered as she and Eloise moved from the fabric to the pattern drawers. "Before we go through all of these, which ones are the least popular? I'm figuring she'd want to hide it where no one would look."

"Evening gowns," said Ree. "Or corsets."

"Men's suits," added Brian. "I saw a fascinating exhibit on men's suitcraft at a textile museum once. Not for the fainthearted."

"Close," chuckled Maisie. "Men's jackets, actually. Really complicated to sew. Try there first."

Suddenly, MJ got up and strode to the front window. Leaning around Vivienne, the display mannequin, she plucked a book out of the beaded satchel that hung from her shoulder.

"Found it!" She held up a smooth, dusky-blue journal fastened with an elastic ribbon.

Maisie hurried over to her. "Vivienne had it all this time. I never would have thought to look there."

"Amazing! How did you figure it out?" Cherry asked.

"I tried to think where I'd hide a journal without anyone in the shop seeing me. The window display sprang to mind."

"Brilliant," said Bev as they all gathered around. "What does it say?"

MJ flipped through the pages covered with Margot's sprawling cursive script. "A lot."

Maisie peered over her shoulder. Most of the notes were written in full sentences, but there were some single words dotted here and there. Others had been circled or Margot had drawn a star beside them. There were sketches too, rough and hastily done in black ballpoint pen.

"How about I make us some coffee, and maybe one of us can read it aloud?" she suggested.

"I'll do it," Ree volunteered, walking over to the head of the table. "I'm an expert at deciphering illegible handwriting, and Margot's isn't that bad."

Once Maisie had poured everyone a brew, they huddled around Ree and the journal.

"Page one," she said in her schoolteacher voice. "*Meeting with Drew Buckland at the Historical Society. Thistle Grove was founded by Silas Penrose and Augustus Rutherford. Partnership. Rutherford = land, Penrose = capital. Descendants still live locally.*"

"We know that," Bev said.

"I didn't," Eloise said.

Ree scanned the rest of the page. "There are a few more names here. Harriet and William Rutherford, Greg Penrose, June and William Penrose."

"The founding families," Maisie murmured. At Cherry's surprised look, she added, "I learned about them today at the historical society too."

"She mentioned a few local businesses too," Ree continued. "Rutherford Timber and Land Management, and Sycamore Hill Golf Estate."

Bev nodded. "That's the basic history of our town, as I was taught it."

"Agreed," said Brian with a nod.

"There's something else," added Ree. "The word 'fire' has a big circle around it."

"Like in the tapestry?" MJ asked, her eyebrows rising.

"Drew Buckland told me about that," Maisie said. "There was a family called Hollowell, I believe, who bought Sycamore Hill. Tragically, their baby was abducted, after which their house burned down in a fire. Ada Hollowell died."

Bev gave a slow nod. "Actually, I remember hearing about that. It happened while I was at the police academy in Salem but it made national news. Wasn't she some Hollywood starlet?"

"That's right," Maisie said. "Her husband was a film director."

Ree pursed her lips. "I took a sabbatical from teaching when my children were young, and we went to California to stay with my sister. That was forty years ago or so, but I heard about it when I got back. Everyone was talking about it."

"My mother told me about it once," Brian recalled. "A baby vanishing into thin air and then the mother dying. It shocked a lot of people, from what I understand."

"Sounds terrible," muttered MJ.

"Before I was born," Eloise said with a shrug.

"Long before," Cherry added with a smile.

"Is there anything in the journal about the kidnapping or the fire?" Maisie asked, nodding to the diary. Ree turned the page but shook her head.

"No, that's the end of her notes from Drew Buckland. The next few pages are about the founding of the town. A few sketches, like the sawmill and the church." She paused and looked up. "Now, this is interesting."

"What?" Cherry demanded.

The whole group leaned in.

"There's a page with a heading that says, 'Father Tom Butterfield.' Underneath, she's written two words: 'baby' and 'land deal.'"

Ree held up the page so they could see.

"Well, baby could be Tobias, but I have no idea what land deal means?" Maisie pondered as they all tried to get a closer look.

"What if she found out something about the kidnapping?" MJ whispered.

Ree flipped ahead, the pages rustling. "If she did, she didn't write it down."

"Father Tom." Cherry narrowed her gaze. "If Margot put him in her notebook, whatever she found must be important." She turned to Maisie. "What do you say we pay Father Tom a visit?"

St. Paul's Episcopal Church was a twenty-minute walk from Tangled Threads, and with the evening so mild and light still lingering in the sky, they decided to stroll there together.

The church itself, built not long after Thistle Grove was founded, was a cheerful white building with a black peaked roof and a modest steeple. It sat on a wide, grassy lawn rimmed with daffodils, right across from the tree-lined stretch of Founders Park.

By the time the Knit and Natter circle wandered up the path and gathered outside, it was already past seven o'clock and the church doors were firmly locked.

"Let's try the rectory," Ree suggested, leading the others down the sidewalk toward the priest's residence.

"Are you sure?" Maisie said, not wanting to intrude.

"Of course. He won't mind."

Maisie glanced at Bev, who shrugged.

Father Tom Butterfield lived in a modest, two-story house built in the same style as the church.

Ree knocked on the front door. Maisie was happy to let her take the lead, since she'd been in Thistle Grove for the longest out of all of them, and knew Father Tom.

The door was opened by a white-haired man in his mid-sixties. He had a slightly stooped build and was dressed in a pair of slacks and a grandfatherly cardigan.

"Good evening." He scratched his head as he studied their little group. "I'm sorry, did we have an appointment?"

"We did not," Ree confirmed. "But we have something we need to ask you. I told them you wouldn't mind."

"Oh, hello Ree. Of course I don't mind."

"Sorry to drop in on you like this," Maisie added. "We'd like to talk to you about our friend, Margot. She... died recently."

Father Tom's face softened into a look of sympathy and he held open the door. "Come on in."

They stepped into a wide entryway.

"This way." Father Tom led them into the living room.

"Please, take a seat." He gestured to a pair of couches that faced each other over a low coffee table. The room was carpeted and warmly lit, thanks to a lamp and the glow of the gas fireplace. There was no television, but the canned laughter of a sitcom floated through from elsewhere in the house.

They crowded onto the two sofas, except for Eloise who was studying a globe on a small coffee table in the corner.

Father Tom remained standing.

"Can I offer anyone tea or coffee? Or a glass of water?"

"No thank you, Tom," Ree said. "Do you mind if we talk about Margot?"

Father Tom folded his hands in front of him. Maisie could imagine him standing at the lectern in front of his congregation.

"I imagine this is about her passing?"

Maisie nodded. "Amongst other things."

"If you need comfort, I'm happy talk about where she might be now. At peace."

"Er, not exactly." Maisie cast a quick look at the others.

"Oh?" He blinked, mild curiosity flickering in his eyes. "What is it, then?"

"Margot came to see you about the tapestry she was making," Maisie began. "For the anniversary?"

He nodded slowly. "Yes, she did drop by to speak with me."

"Could you tell us what you talked about?"

He shifted, tugging the sleeves of his sweater down. "A number of things, really. She was researching the town's history, as you know."

"Yes, we found her journal," MJ said. "She mentioned meeting with you, but there was also some stuff we couldn't quite make sense of."

His brow creased. "What sort of stuff?"

"Something about a baby, and some sort of land deal," MJ said.

Father Tom stared at her for a long beat. He seemed caught off-guard at the statement.

Eventually, he cleared his throat. "She asked me about the founding of St. Paul's, after which I showed her the church records. The land the town sits on was donated by Augustus Rutherford, and generous funding by Silas Penrose allowed the construction of the church. She could have meant that?"

"Could see those records?" Maisie asked, thinking about the upside down cross.

Father Tom hesitated, but only for a split second. "Of course. It will take some time, however, as I will have to dig them out of the archives."

"Thank you." Maisie said.

"Do you think the baby could be Tobias Hollowell?" Cherry asked. "We know about the kidnapping and the fire."

He sighed, dropping his head. "That was a very dark time in our town's history."

"Margot asked me to finish the tapestry," Maisie said. "But I can't do that unless I know what she was going to put in it."

"I see." He thought for a moment. "Well, Margot asked for Tobias Hollowell's church records."

Eloise glanced at her mother, excitedly.

"What kind of records?" Ree asked.

"Baptism. I performed the ceremony myself." He gave a pained expression like the memory physically hurt him.

"That must have been just before he was taken," Maisie surmised.

He nodded. "The child was only a few weeks old when it happened. The parents had moved into the area a few years before, from Hollywood. Ada was an actress, and quite a good one at that. He was a film director. They came to get away from the limelight."

"And bought Sycamore Hill," Maisie added.

"That's right. Tobias was born a few years later. Sweet child."

"He was taken during a party?" MJ asked, wanting confirmation from the priest.

Father Tom gave a sad nod. "There was a massive search. The whole town came to help, but baby Tobias was never found."

Cherry shook her head. "It's so strange. Nobody had any idea who took him?"

Father Tom flattened his lips. "Nope, the mystery of his disappearance was never solved. The parents were devastated, obviously, and Ada took to her room and didn't come out. That's where she was when the fire broke out."

"How long after the kidnapping was the fire?" MJ asked.

"I can't recall exactly, but I think it was only a few months."

"What happened to Robert, the film director?" Maisie asked.

Father Tom gave a sad shake of his head. "He left town. Sold Sycamore Hill to the Penrose family. I suppose he couldn't bear to stay there. Can't blame him, really."

"Did you tell this to Margot?" Maisie asked him. Father Tom had elaborated on the story Drew Buckland had told her, but there wasn't a lot here they didn't already know.

"Yes, but I begged her not to put those gory details into the tapestry. It's not a time anyone wants to remember."

Maisie met MJ's gaze.

But she had.

The small figure in the flames must be Ada Hollowell and the baby must be tiny Tobias.

But what did they have to do with Margot's murder?

Chapter 6

Unfinished Business

The conversation with Father Tom kept circling in Maisie's mind as she went about her day at Tangled Threads. Mondays were always quiet at the shop, giving her plenty of room to think while she arranged new merchandise, straightened displays, and helped the handful of customers who wandered in for a browse.

If they were going to trace Margot's footsteps, they had to see both the land records and the baptism certificate that she'd requested. Before she forgot, she messaged Brian to follow up. As the local librarian, he'd be familiar with church records, and be able to nudge Father Tom to dig them out, as he put it.

All the while, her thoughts drifted back to the Hollowell family tragedy. How long had the search gone on? Were there any real clues? Had anyone ever been considered a suspect in the baby's disappearance?

And why, of all things, had Margot woven it into her tapestry?

By one o'clock, Maisie decided she needed to step outside. She'd already finished the sandwich she'd packed from home, but all that turning things over in her mind had left her with a light throb behind her temples. A walk into town, and a bit of mild spring air, would do her good.

"Want to join me?" she asked Mewsly as she flipped the *Out for Lunch* sign against the door. Her long, brightly patterned skirt swished around her ankle boots, and she slipped on a light spring jacket over her cream sweater.

From her basket by the yarn display, Mewsly extended one front leg, splayed her toes, and stretched her claws. Then, with a slow blink at Maisie, tucked her paw neatly back beneath her body.

"I love you too," Maisie said with a smile. "See you after my walk."

Warm spring air greeted her as she stepped outside onto the sidewalk. She loved the way the sunlight flickered through the fresh green leaves that had appeared along Main Street.

Hands tucked loosely into her jacket pockets, she set off down the street, determined to clear her head.

Not entirely sure where she was going, she wandered past the cheerful row of shops, wine-tasting rooms, restaurants, and teashops that lined the street. Some of them she recognized from Margot's tapestry.

There was the historic Thistle Grove Hotel, a tall, square building nearly as old as the town itself. The aroma of tomato sauce and warm garlic bread hit her from the popular Italian place on the corner and despite having eaten, her stomach rumbled.

Crossing Main, she decided to stroll toward Founders Park. The park was one of her favorite spots in any season with its century-old oaks and towering Douglas firs, but something about it always felt especially welcoming in spring.

Children played along the paths, dog walkers waved as they passed, and the stone fountain in the center tinkled merrily as people tossed in lucky pennies. Main Street might have been the town's bustling hub, she thought, but Founders Park—the peaceful pocket of green framed by historic buildings—was its heart.

She stood beneath the trees listening to the leaves rustle and admired the gentle charm of the neighborhood surrounding them. Quite by chance, her gaze wandered to the two-story, Queen Anne–style home that stood directly across the park from the church.

Penrose House.

The stately home now served as Thistle Grove's town hall. Nearly as old as St. Paul's, it featured a peaked roof, a formal front porch, and a row of columns stretching along the veranda. The building had been carefully maintained over the years, ever since the second generation of Penroses donated it to the town.

A thought struck her. The town hall might hold records, something about the Hollowells, or the fire that had upended their lives.

Stepping into Penrose House felt like walking onto a carefully preserved set from the early twentieth century. She paused just inside the door, taking in the bell-shaped chandelier, the carved wooden furniture, and the original porcelain door handles—details that had been chosen with care and left undisturbed.

The reception area felt welcoming, with its polished wooden floors and clean white walls. It was set up for residents to speak with the receptionist or sit and wait for their appointments with whichever public official they needed.

A bronze plaque on the wall laid out the building's design. The mayor's and deputy mayor's offices, the council chambers, and the council secretary were all down the corridor to the right, while the town treasurer and the facilities department sat to the left.

Maisie approached the receptionist, a cheerful young man in horn-rimmed glasses seated behind a shiny wooden desk. The American flag stood behind him on its brass stand, and a large, nostalgic painting of Main Street in the early 1900s hung on the wall, giving the room a welcoming, old-world charm.

"Can I help you?" he enquired politely.

"I hope so." Maisie shifted her gaze away from the historic scene on the wall. "I'm trying to find out about an event that happened in Thistle Grove about forty years ago."

The young man gave an apologetic head shake. "I'm sorry. We don't keep historical records here. But there are a few places in town that might be able to help. Have you tried the Historical Society? The Public Library still has a microfiche collection if you're feeling adventurous."

"I've been to the Historical Society," Maisie told him. "I'm looking for information about the Sycamore Hill estate."

Brian could visit the library's microfiche collection. That would be right up his alley.

His face brightened. "Ah, Sycamore Hill. Well, I can at

least tell you who owns it now—William and June Penrose. They're descendants of Silas Penrose, one of our founding fathers. Their son, in fact, is our very own Mayor Penrose."

She smiled at his enthusiasm. "Thank you, but I'm particularly interested in the couple who owned it before they did. The Hollowells, was it?"

His face fell. "That was before my time, I'm afraid, but Rutherford Timber and Land Management keep a lot of the old land records. They might have something that could help you."

"Interested in the past, are we?" interrupted a warm baritone.

Maisie swung around to find a handsome man in his thirties standing behind her. His mouth was curved into a polite but contained smile. It didn't meet his eyes.

The receptionist perked up. "Perfect timing. Allow me to introduce Mayor Greg Penrose."

Penrose was tall, with expressive blue eyes and thick brown hair neatly combed back from his face. His navy-blue suit was crisp, his shirt collar white, and his shoes polished to a high shine. She had to admire how effortlessly put together he was.

He extended a hand. "I don't believe we've met."

"Actually, we have, Mr. Mayor," Maisie said. "I'm Maisie Button, the owner of Tangled Threads, the craft store on Main Street."

His smile didn't falter. "Ah. Yes, of course. My apologies."

"That's okay. You must meet so many people."

He gave a self-deprecating nod. "Occupational hazard, I'm afraid."

"I was a friend of Margot Bellamy," she added, before she lost his attention. His eyes were already beginning to drift. "I have her unfinished tapestry, the one she was creating for the town's anniversary before she died."

He gave a somber nod. "I heard about what happened. I'm sorry for your loss."

"Thank you," she murmured.

"I wondered what had become of the tapestry." He stroked his square jaw. "It was to be an important piece for our anniversary collection."

Maisie nodded. "It still could be. Margot asked me to complete it."

"Excellent." He drew his hands together as in prayer. "We appreciate your goodwill gesture, Ms. Button. Please let me know if there is anything I can do to help."

He was very charming, if a little insincere. But she could see why he was popular with the residents of Thistle Grove.

"Actually, now that you mention it... I'm trying to understand some of the designs she used. In particular, Sycamore Hill, which I understand belongs to your family?"

"Ah, yes. You're correct. My parents bought it some time ago, shortly after I was born."

"Terrible what happened there." Maisie led him away from the receptionist, who was still hanging on to every word.

"Tragic but not forgotten." He gestured to a bronze plaque on the wall. "Have you seen our memorial plaque?"

Maisie walked over to examine it. Etched into the polished metal was a commemoration of the life of Ada Hollowell and her son, Tobias. It read: *In Memoriam. Ada Hollowell. b. 1953 – d. 1985. Tobias Hollowell. b. 1984. This plaque honors the lives of Ada Hollowell, actress, and her infant son, Tobias. Taken too soon. Always in our hearts.*

"That's a lovely memorial," she said.

He straightened his tie. "My family commissioned it. My parents knew the Hollowells, you see. It's not much, but they wanted something to remember them by."

"I'm surprised your parents purchased the property after what happened there," Maisie mused.

Penrose stiffened. "Have you visited the Sycamore Hill estate? My parents completely transformed the property. It's nothing like it once was."

"I've driven past a couple of times," Maisie admitted, her gaze still on the plaque. "But I've never visited in person. I want to, though."

"You should. It's one of the top golfing destinations in the state."

Maisie got back on track. "Do you know why Margot would want to include what happened on the tapestry?"

Penrose started, his careful façade momentarily crumbling. "She what?"

"There are hints of a fire and a young baby in the design. I was just trying to understand why."

"There are?" Annoyance marred his handsome features. "I have no idea why she'd do that. It's not very appropriate. Not at all. Perhaps you can alter it?"

"It is part of the town's history, is it not?" Maisie asked.

"I don't want it in there." He cleared his throat. "It's an anniversary commemoration. My family, along with the Rutherfords founded this town. I won't see their name sullied."

Maisie blinked, surprised by his outburst.

He seemed to recover himself, but remained tense. "I'm sorry. That was a terrible time in our history, and I won't allow rumors to become engrained in our town's legacy."

"Rumors?" asked Maisie.

He hesitated. "It was said Ada Holloway was a bad mother. Neglectful."

Maisie pursed her lips. "Really? Do you know why?"

He shook his head. "I only know what people have told me. Now, if you'll excuse me. I have another appointment."

"Thank you for your time."

He nodded, his jaw tight, and strode away.

Now that was interesting.

Had Margot spoken to the Penroses? Had she uncovered some dark secret about baby Tobias's kidnapping, or a tragic tale of neglect? Was that why she'd put those symbols in the tapestry?

Leaving the town hall, Maisie felt a glimmer of hope. Like she was finally on the right track.

What they needed to do now was learn more about Ada Hollowell and the kidnapping of baby Tobias.

Chapter 7

The Inside Story

Maisie had just finished helping a customer color-match some thread to a beloved shirt that needed repair when her phone rang. She made her way past the tapestry loom, now positioned at the back of the store, to answer.

"You busy?" Ree asked.

"Not really. Just had to navigate my way around Margot's loom. It's taking up so much space, but the customers love it. It's become a real talking piece."

"I'm sure." Ree chuckled. "Speaking of Margot, I have a lead for us."

"You do?" They needed one. She'd been so busy she hadn't had a chance to look into the kidnapping or the fire that had destroyed the Hollowell mansion.

"I do. A friend of mine knows the maid who worked for

the Hollowells back when everything happened. She was there the day the baby disappeared."

"You're kidding!" Maisie exclaimed. "And she's willing to talk to us?"

"She is, but my friend says she was badly shaken by what happened. It might be best if just the two of us speak with her, rather than bringing the whole knitting circle."

"Absolutely," Maisie agreed, trying to contain her excitement. "That's completely understandable." She glanced up at the clock positioned behind the register. "Is she local? Would she be able to stop by the store this evening after closing? Maybe around five-thirty?"

"That only gives us half an hour before the others turn up," Ree reminded her.

"I know, but you're very good at keeping people occupied if we need a little more time."

Ree gave a soft laugh. "All right. I'll ask her."

They said their goodbyes and ended the call.

Maisie let out a long breath and turned toward the tapestry. The muted colors seemed to glow softly under the lamp at the back of the shop. There was something quietly expectant about it, as though it were waiting. Waiting for them to figure out its secrets.

Maybe the Hollowells' maid could finally shed some light on what had happened.

The sun had dipped below the rooftops by the time Maisie finally flipped the window sign to *Closed*.

Outside, the street glowed beneath strings of warm fairy lights that stayed up year-round, giving Main Street a gentle, welcoming shimmer as evening settled in.

Mewsly had slipped out earlier in the afternoon but had returned well before dusk, paws dusty from some secret expedition. Now she was curled up in her basket by the yarn display, contentedly digesting her dinner.

The bell above the door chimed as Ree arrived with the former maid.

Right on time.

"Maisie, this is Glynis," Ree said, introducing a slim woman in her seventies, draped in a light knitted shawl.

The woman nodded, a little uncertain.

"Welcome," Maisie said warmly, going up to her and shaking her hand. "Thank you for agreeing to speak with us."

"You're welcome, dear." Glynis stepped inside a little farther and glanced around the shop, eyes widening as she took in the colorful displays of fabric and yarn.

"You have a wonderful store. I've always wanted to come in here, but I never had a reason. I don't sew or knit, you see."

"It's never too late to learn." Maisie gave an encouraging smile and gestured toward the table. "Please, make yourself comfortable. Would you like a coffee?"

"Do you have tea?"

"Of course. Apple-cinnamon, mint, chamomile, or plain old regular?"

Glynis's shoulders relaxed. "A chamomile tea would be lovely. Thank you."

"I'll put the coffee on for us," Ree told Maisie with a knowing look as she moved toward the beverage station. "Trust me, you're going to want a strong cup."

By the time Maisie returned with the steaming mug of chamomile, Glynis was seated and gazing up at the Proud Projects board. It was a cheerful patchwork of photographs.

Tiny baby sweaters, puffball beanies, a quilted tote bag, and an exceptionally blue prom dress a determined mum had stitched for her daughter.

"These are wonderful," Glynis said, accepting her tea with a nod. "It must be lovely to make something like that."

"They really are." Maisie settled into the chair opposite her. "You'd be welcome at one of our Knit and Natter nights, or the Sew Something circle on Saturday mornings. We're a friendly bunch, and we teach beginners all the basics."

"Oh, I don't know." Glynis flushed a little. "I'd be all thumbs."

"Everyone is at first. You should've seen the outfits I made for my childhood dog. A pillowcase with holes in it would have been an improvement."

Glynis chuckled, and Ree—who'd taken the seat beside her—laughed too.

"I wasn't much better," the retired schoolteacher admitted. "My first knitting project? I ripped the whole thing out. Twice."

Glynis winced. "Oh dear."

"It happens to everyone," Maisie assured her. "Sometimes you make a mistake you just can't fix, so you unravel the whole thing and start fresh."

The coffee maker sputtered, and Ree jumped up. By the time she returned with their coffees, Glynis seemed more at ease and ready to talk.

"Ree tells me you used to work for the Hollowells," Maisie began, prompting her gently.

Glynis nodded, her hands wrapped around the mug.

"It was a long time ago now," she said. "But yes. I was their maid from the moment they moved here, almost."

"How did you get the job?" Maisie asked. "Did you know who they were at the time?"

She gave a soft snort. "No, I had no idea they were this famous movie star couple. I answered an ad in the newspaper and, well, I was pretty dumbfounded when I found out. I'd never worked for anyone so well known before."

"Did you interview at the house?" Maisie asked.

"Oh, yes. And my eyes just about popped out of my head when I saw Sycamore Hill." She gave a fond smile at the memory. "What a beautiful home. A mansion, really. There were six bedrooms, and just as many bathrooms. A study, a music room with a grand piano, and a great old dining room with the most gorgeous crystal chandelier." She laughed. "You don't forget a thing like that. Especially since I had to climb a ladder to dust it!"

"Did they pay you well?" Ree asked.

Glynis nodded. "Oh, yes. The Hollowells were very generous. Wonderful people too. Ada was so glamorous. Slender and graceful. She told me once she'd been a dancer before she went into films."

Maisie nodded, already assembling the details in her mind the way she would for a character. She could see Ada taking shape piece by piece, each detail settling into place.

"She wore silk pantsuits," Glynis went on, "and her makeup was always perfect."

Maisie pictured clean lines, soft movement in the fabric, and a woman who knew exactly how to present herself the moment she stepped into a room.

"I heard a rumor," Maisie began carefully, "that she wasn't a very good mother. Is there any truth to that, in your opinion?"

Glynis looked horrified. "Oh, gosh. None at all. That child couldn't have had a more doting mother."

Maisie frowned. That wasn't what she'd heard from the mayor. She didn't like inconsistencies. It either meant someone was mistaken, or someone was lying.

"There wasn't anything Ada wouldn't do for that child," Glynis continued, more animated than Maisie had seen her. "I helped them set up the nursery. Ada wanted it done up in a circus theme. The wallpaper had lions and tigers and cute little clowns, and Robert bought a big, beautiful wooden crib with a ruffled canopy. Quilted bumpers too, although you wouldn't have those these days."

It sure sounded like Ada wanted the best for her little boy.

"What was he like, the husband?" Ree asked.

"Oh, he was a doll," Glynis said fondly. "Handsome and charming. Protective too. He interviewed me first, wanted to know all about me and my family. He asked whether I liked going to the movies, or if I followed the goings-on in Hollywood. I said I didn't follow the news much, not with two of my own to run after, and he seemed satisfied with that."

She chuckled. "It was only later that I realized he wanted to be sure I wouldn't sell them out to the papers. I never dreamed of it, of course."

"Of course," Maisie echoed. "Glynis, can you tell us about the day Tobias disappeared?"

Her smile faded. "Poor Ada. She only had him a few weeks. Baby Tobias. What a sweet, precious thing."

"How did it happen?" Ree asked, leaning forward. "Were you there when he was kidnapped?"

Glynis nodded and took a shuddering breath. Ree patted her hand.

"There was a party—a garden party—at the house,"

Glynis said finally. "Ada wanted to see people again. Have a little fun."

"She wanted to do something that made her feel like her old self again after the baby," Maisie said, giving a nod of understanding.

"That's right. It wasn't a late-night affair, or anything scandalous. Just a small gathering at their home in the middle of the afternoon."

"How many guests?" Maisie asked.

Glynis thought for a moment. "Maybe twenty. Thirty, at most. Everyone mingled on the lawn in the sunshine. It was a beautiful day, I remember that. There were canapes and drinks—the usual fare for a party like that."

"Who was looking after Tobias?" asked Maisie.

"His nanny, Lynda. Lynda Tanner. He made a brief appearance with Ada when everyone arrived, but then the nanny took him off for a nap."

"So, when did they realize he was gone?"

"A short time later." Glynis took a heavy breath. "I was outside clearing plates, when Lynda came running out. She was hysterical. Screaming that she couldn't find Tobias anywhere. He'd gone."

"Gone?" Ree repeated.

"Yes, snatched from the nursery. After Robert managed to calm her down, she told him she'd stepped out of the room to fetch something, that she was only gone for five minutes, if that. When she got back, he was missing."

Maisie frowned. "Was there a ransom note? Any sign of a break-in?"

"No, nothing like that," Glynis said, wringing her hands. "I mean, the house was open, so anyone could have walked in."

"On account of the party," Maisie surmised.

She nodded.

"How about you?" Maisie pressed. "Were you limited to the kitchen and garden area?"

Glynis blinked, momentarily off guard. "Me? I was mostly on the terrace. But I went in and out through the back. The kitchen was just inside the doors."

"But normally?" she asked.

"Normally I had the run of the house," Glynis explained. "It was my responsibility to keep the place clean and tidy."

"Of course." Maisie didn't like pressing her when she was so clearly upset, but the fact remained. Glynis also had opportunity, as Bev would say. She'd had access to the house and could have disappeared in those five minutes to secret baby Tobias out and hand him to a waiting third party. Was it likely? Not from what Maisie could see. But it was a possibility they had to consider.

"What happened next?" she asked.

"We searched everywhere. The house, the gardens, even into the wood. Even some the guests helped, but we couldn't find him. The sheriff was called, of course, and he and his deputies questioned everyone, but no one had seen anything." She shook her head, unshed tears welling in her eyes. "Ada was inconsolable. I never saw her again after that."

"They fired you?" Ree asked, shocked.

"Oh, no. I still worked there, but it wasn't the same after that. Ada took to her room. They say she had a breakdown, poor thing. Can't blame her, really. The rumors didn't help."

"Rumors?" Maisie asked.

Glynis bit her lip. "People were saying it was Ada's fault for neglecting him. How could she throw a party with a newborn at home? Those Hollywood types, always drinking and carrying on. You know how it goes."

Maisie nodded. Unfortunately, she did.

"There were even rumors she'd killed the child herself and staged the disappearance."

"How awful," Ree whispered.

"Of course, it was all lies." Glynis looked up, a spark of anger behind the tears. "She was at the party the whole time, talking and laughing with the guests. I saw her myself."

"What did the sheriff say?" Maisie asked.

"I wasn't privy to that," Glynis said with a little shrug. "I do know Robert was working with them, cooperating as best he could. I heard him on the phone, demanding answers. Nothing came of it."

Maisie suppressed a shiver. It suddenly felt cold in the craft store. What an awful thing to have happened.

"That's not all," Ree murmured, taking Glynis's hand. "Tell her about the fire."

"Oh, Lord. The fire," Glynis whispered, her expression haunted. This was dredging up some tough memories for her.

"Can you tell us about that day?" Maisie asked.

"It happened at night, so I wasn't there. I found out the next day. Everyone in town was talking about it. You could see the smoke for miles. The whole house had burned to the ground."

"And Ada lost her life," Maisie added.

"That's right. Robert barely got out alive, so I was told. They blamed her for that too. People said she must have been smoking in bed. She kept her bedroom door locked because she wanted to be alone, so Robert couldn't get in to save her." She wiped away a tear.

"I'm so sorry," Maisie murmured.

Ree squeezed Glynis's hand.

"I'm sorry. Talking about it brings it all back."

"Did they investigate the fire?" Ree asked.

"I don't know," Glynis sniffed. "No arrests were ever made. Not over what happened to little Tobias, or the fire."

"They couldn't have found anything," Maisie surmised.

Glynis took a shaky breath. "Not long after that, Robert moved away, and the land was bought by the Penrose family. They built their golf course there. The news story faded, and everyone tried to forget the tragedy."

"Not everyone," Maisie mused. Margot had brought it back and put it in her tapestry. Maisie was more certain than ever that's what had gotten her killed.

Now they just had to figure out why.

Chapter 8

A New Lead

Shortly after Glynis had left, the door swung open and Cherry walked in with her daughter close behind.

"Perfect timing," Ree said with a grin.

Cherry brushed a hand proudly through her daughter's wind-tousled hair. "Guess what? El found a new lead."

Maisie looked up, interest sparking. "Really?"

"We could use one," Ree said as she gathered the empty mugs and carried them toward the kitchenette. While talking with Glynis had been enlightening, it hadn't brought them any closer to the truth.

"Do you want to share now or wait until the others get here?" Maisie asked Eloise, gesturing for her to take a seat at the table.

"The others are here," Brian called as he stepped inside, holding the door for Bev and MJ. Both women had light spring jackets pulled around them against the mild evening breeze. "What did we miss?"

"Eloise has something to tell us," Maisie announced as the new arrivals slipped off their jackets and settled in.

Eloise, bouncing on her toes, looked as if she might burst with excitement.

"Go ahead," Maisie said, smiling.

"Okay. So I was looking through Mom's photos on her phone. I wanted to see if I could find more clues, and I did." She glanced toward the back of the store. "Maisie, can I show them on the tapestry?"

"Sure. Come on over." They all got up and moved over to where the tapestry loom stood. The vibrant golds and greens and the rich reds, browns, and creams of Margot's work glowed softly.

Eloise pointed to the squiggles woven into the border that framed the scene. "These aren't just weird lines. There are letters hiding in there. Look. Over here you can see a 'T' and an 'H'."

Everyone leaned in. Brian and Ree put on their glasses.

"I see it!" blurted out MJ. "She's right. I think they're initials."

"Excellent job, El," Ree said.

Bev tilted a smile at the teen. "Nice work, detective."

Eloise beamed. "Thanks, but who is TH?"

"Tobias Hollowell," Everyone said in unison.

"The missing baby?" Eloise whispered.

Maisie drew in a breath. "Okay, let's grab a hot beverage and share what we've discovered so far."

Once everyone was armed with a mug of something warm, they resettled around the farmhouse table. Eloise opted to sit on the floor beside Mewsly.

"I don't want to steal Eloise's thunder," Brian began,

shooting the girl a fond look, "but I think I've also found something."

"Do tell," Maisie urged, as they all glanced over at him.

He held up his phone where he'd zoomed in on the section of the tapestry that depicted the town hall and Founders Park.

"It might be nothing, but the trees on either side of the town hall should be oaks or Douglas firs. Founders Park is famous for them."

"Yes, they are," Maisie agreed. "I stood under them the other day. Besides, the ground is littered with acorns in the fall."

MJ had risen out of her chair and was scrutinizing the photograph on Brian's phone. "The colors are off."

"Exactly," he said with a grin. "That's because they're not oaks or firs, they're sycamores." He pointed to the trunks. "Sycamore trunks are patchy. The bark falls away and leaves spots of green and white. It's unmistakable."

"He's right," Ree said, frowning.

MJ walked back to the tapestry. "You're right. These are definitely sycamores," she called from the back of the store.

"What do sycamores have to do with anything?" Cherry asked, as MJ returned to the table. "Why would Margot swap out the oak trees?"

"To point us to Sycamore Hill," Maisie said, placing both hands flat on the table. "That's where the baby disappeared. That's where the fire was that ended Ada Hollowell's life."

"Then that's where the answer must lie," Ree stated.

Maisie ran a hand through her hair. "Except I spoke to Mayor Penrose the other day and he told me his parents had completely transformed the property. There's no point in inspecting it now, forty years later."

"That's true," Cherry agreed. "It's totally different now. The main house isn't even on the same spot as the Hollowells."

"We interviewed a friend of Ree's who worked as a maid for the Hollowells," Maisie confided.

They all turned to face her, except Ree, who picked up the story. "Yes, Glynis told us what happened."

At the expectant looks, Ree filled them in on the party, the location out on the lawn, the baby in his nursery, and Lynda stepping out for ten minutes to take care of some laundry.

"That's when he was taken," she concluded.

"The sheriff was called," Maisie added, "but he didn't find anything."

"Any suspects?" Bev asked.

"Glynis didn't know the details of the investigation," Maisie told her. "She said Ada was a good mother, but everyone blamed her for the abduction, basically saying it was her fault."

"How could it have been her fault?" MJ argued.

"It must have been devastating," Cherry added, glancing at her own daughter, now stroking a loudly purring Mewsly.

"Glynis also said that Ada didn't come out of her room after that," Maisie added. "Apparently, she kept the door to her bedroom locked."

"That's what killed her," Ree explained. She looked gravely around the table. "When the house went up in flames, Robert couldn't get her out. The rumor mill blamed Ada for that too, saying she must have been smoking in bed."

"Unbelievable," sputtered Cherry, shaking her bright red bob.

"That's so unfair." MJ's hands were balled into fists on the table.

"And really sad," Brian added.

"Let's summarize the information we've got so far." Bev set down her coffee mug and took a deep breath. "Margot was working on a tapestry for the town's anniversary. She was looking into the history of the town, in particular the kidnapping of baby Tobias and the fire at Sycamore Hill. We don't know why, yet, but it stands to reason that something she found out got her killed."

"Don't forget she changed the design of the tapestry." MJ sat up straight.

"And forgot her notebook here at the store," Cherry added.

"Accidentally on purpose," Eloise chimed in.

"Then there's her plea to Maisie to finish the tapestry, if anything happened to her," said Brian casting a significant look around the table. "She knew she was in danger."

Bev gave a firm nod. "I agree with Brian. Margot stumbled onto something that someone didn't want getting out. Whatever it was, it made her a target."

"We can assume that whatever she discovered is linked to Tobias Hollowell and the fire at Sycamore Hill," Maisie finished, voicing what had been bouncing through her head the last few days. "The clues are in the tapestry."

"Don't forget the church records that Father Tom is going to give us," Brian added.

"The question is, what did she find out?" Ree glanced around the table.

"She found out the truth," Maisie concluded. "Whatever that was."

Chapter 9

A Clearer Picture

Lynda Tanner, who had once been baby Tobias's nanny, was just shy of sixty and lived only a few towns over from Thistle Grove. Brian, who loved a good research project almost as much as he loved a fresh cup of coffee, had volunteered to poke around in old census records and phone listings. True to form, he'd managed to track her down by the very next day.

Ree, thinking a familiar name might put Lynda at ease, asked Glynis if she would reach out. It took a bit of gentle coaxing, but eventually Glynis convinced Lynda to meet with Maisie and Bev.

A soft glow lingered in the sky as Maisie waited in front of Bev's house for her to come out. It was a little past six, and the town was wrapped in that gentle, blue-tinged light that comes just before dusk.

Bev stepped out of her light gray Cape Cod–style house a moment later, her mustard-yellow spring jacket bright against the soft evening hue. She slipped into the passenger seat and set her travel mug of coffee into the center cupholder.

"How do you want to play this?" the former sheriff asked as they made their way out of Thistle Grove and toward the interstate. Lynda's home was only fifteen minutes east.

Maisie laughed. "You sound like a TV detective."

Bev gave a modest shrug. "Well, I've learned it helps to have some sort of plan before you walk into an interview."

"As long as we're both the good cops," Maisie joked, giving Bev a sideways smile. Then she sobered a little. "When Ree and I talked with Glynis, she got emotional, even after forty years. Let's just see how things feel with Lynda. Whoever she connects with best can do most of the talking."

"Good call," Bev agreed. "You're wonderful with people, Maisie. Was that a big part of your job back in LA?"

Maisie lifted a shoulder. "Sort of. I worked closely with actors and directors to bring everything together."

"Do you miss it?" Bev asked. "All that Hollywood sparkle?"

Maisie thought for a moment. "I loved the creative work. It was my happy place. But the long hours... the travel... being away from home all the time. That's the part I don't miss."

"So you're enjoying your quieter life here in Thistle Grove?"

"It was quiet," Maisie said with a scoff. "Until all this started. I never imagined I'd be investigating a murder in Thistle Grove."

Bev gave a dry chuckle. "You'd be surprised. Small towns see their fair share of

crime. But most of the cases I handled were heat-of-the-moment things. Someone loses their temper, someone makes a bad decision." She shook her head. "But this? A murder tangled up with a forty-year-old disappearance. It's a different kind of story."

"Yet here we are," Maisie said as she turned into Lynda's driveway.

The house was a tidy ranch-style bungalow with a neatly mowed lawn and cedar hedges trimmed with care.

She and Bev stepped out of the car and made their way up the front walkway, the mild evening air carrying the faint scent of someone's backyard barbecue down the street.

Maisie pressed the doorbell.

After a moment, a middle-aged man with a kind face, warm eyes, and a full head of silvering hair opened the door.

"You must be Maisie and Bev," he said pleasantly. "I'm Don, Lydia's husband. Come on in."

"Thank you," Maisie said, as they stepped inside.

"Lynda's set out coffee and cake for you in the den."

"That's so thoughtful," Bev said, as they followed him down a hallway lined with family portraits. Maisie noticed smiling girls in matching dresses, graduation caps, holiday snapshots.

"You have a beautiful family," she told Don, who's expression softened.

"Thank you. Our three daughters are all grown now. We're very lucky, though. They've given us a whole brood of grandkids."

The house still had the warm, family feel to it. The lingering smell of that night's pasta sauce hung in the air, and a grandfather clock ticked a solid, comforting rhythm.

They found Lynda in a snug den at the back of the house. A full carrot cake sat proudly on the low table, and beside it was a French-style coffee press along with a little pitcher of cream and a dish of sugar cubes.

Lynda had been sitting in a recliner reading a magazine. She stood when they entered and rubbed her hands on her trousers. A sure sign she was nervous.

"Hi, Lynda. I'm Maisie, we spoke on the phone." Maisie offered her hand with a warm smile. "This is my friend Bev. Thank you so much for seeing us, and"—she nodded toward the cake and coffee—"for going to all this trouble."

Lynda waved her off kindly. "Oh, it wasn't any trouble at all. I needed something to occupy myself until you arrived." She gestured toward the cake. "Since I've made it, can I tempt you with a slice?"

"Absolutely," Maisie said, and Bev chimed in with an enthusiastic nod as the two of them settled onto the couch.

"I think I recognize you, Bev," Lynda said as she picked up the cake knife. "Weren't you the county sheriff once upon a time?"

"I was," Bev said, accepting her slice on a delicate china plate. "And generous icing is always the right choice."

Lynda beamed. "I quite agree. Never skimp on icing." She handed a piece to Maisie. "It's one of my guiding principles."

Maisie laughed. "That's a very good principle. I might adopt it myself."

Lynda poured their coffees.

"We appreciate you talking with us," she added. "I know it was a very painful part of your life."

Lynda kept her eyes on the cake for a beat.

"It was," she said, looking up. "Truly one of the worst things I've ever lived through."

"How long did you work for the Hollowells?" Bev asked, kicking off the questioning.

Lynda sank down on a chair and put her hands in her lap.

"Not very long. They brought me on near the end of the pregnancy, just to help get everything ready. When Tobias was taken—" Her voice faltered, the words catching in her throat. "I'm sorry. I haven't spoken about any of this in decades."

"That's all right," Maisie said, glancing at Bev. "Take your time."

"Well, I left not long after it happened."

"What was it like, working for them?" Bev asked.

Lynda let out a quiet breath. "Honestly, it was a breeze compared to some of my earlier jobs. I babysat all through my teens, and I had one other nannying position, but the Hollowells... they were different."

"In what way?" Maisie asked.

"To start with, they were a lovely couple," Lynda said, her expression softening with memory. "Very charming. Very glamorous. And Tobias was the sweetest baby. He slept through the night almost right away. I hardly had to do more than the usual—changing him, washing his little things, and taking him to Ada for feedings."

"Sounds like an easy job," Maisie noted.

Lynda gave a small, wistful smile. "I loved it. We took so many walks with the stroller. It was one of those old-fashioned perambulators—big and blue and a bit unwieldy. Tobias would look up at the sky and wiggle his little arms, and I'd tell him all about the birds and the clouds and everything he'd get to do once he was old enough to run around and play." She paused, and her eyes filled with tears. "I'm sorry."

"It's all right." Maisie shifted forward and laid a comforting hand on Lynda's arm. "We know this isn't easy."

Lynda sniffled and brushed her eyes with the back of her hand. "Goodness. I knew I should've put a splash of whiskey in this coffee."

"There's still time," Bev said, giving her a teasing grin.

That earned a small laugh from all three of them, and the heavy feeling in the room eased a little.

Maisie let the warmth linger for a moment before easing into the next question. "Do you mind talking about the day of the garden party?"

Lynda released a long, steadying breath but nodded. "I've lived with it for more than forty years. I guess I can talk about it."

"Why don't you start at the beginning?" Bev said. "When did you arrive at the house that day?"

"First thing in the morning," Lynda said. "Ada didn't have a night nanny. She was breastfeeding and preferred to handle the nights herself. By six o'clock she was ready to hand over little Tobias and get a few hours of sleep. We went through our usual morning routine. Bath, getting dressed. The guests weren't coming until after lunch, so we took a walk with the stroller, and then I put him down for his morning nap." She stared passed them, lost in her memories.

"What happened next?" Bev prompted.

"Once he woke up, I took him to Ada for his feeding, and she asked me to dress him in his special outfit for the party. It was a little blue plaid romper." A sad smile tugged at her mouth. "She was excited to show him off to her friends."

"What time did the party start?" Maisie asked.

"Two o'clock," Lynda said with a small, firm nod. "Ada

wanted everyone to meet the baby before his afternoon nap."

Maisie could picture the scene. A new mother proud of her little boy. It was heart wrenching what had happened. "Do you remember who was there?"

"Oh, everyone who was anyone in Thistle Grove was there." Lynda wiggled her eyebrows. "The mayor, the Penroses and the Rutherfords, of course, as well as a handful of celebrity friends from Hollywood."

Bev leaned in a little. "What was the atmosphere like? Was there any tension between the guests?"

Maisie shot Bev a grateful look. Her years of experience were proving useful.

"For the most part, it was cheerful," Lynda said, though a small crease formed between her brows. "Well, except for June Penrose. She was heavily pregnant and due any day. We were a bit worried about her, to be honest. She hadn't been feeling quite herself, if I remember correctly."

Maisie glanced at Bev. "Mayor Penrose told me he hadn't been born yet when Tobias was taken."

"That's right," Lynda said. "But as I recall, she gave birth just a couple of days later."

Maisie nodded. That lined up neatly with everything they'd learned so far.

"There was a live band, and plenty of refreshments," Lynda went on. "Big pitchers of lemonade, and the most wonderfully exotic cocktails."

"Sounds fun," Maisie said. "Was Ada drinking?"

"Oh, no. Not while she was breastfeeding. She was very careful about things like that."

Bev gave a small, approving nod.

"Everyone was having such a nice time," Lynda said,

her gaze drifting off again. "Ada and Robert were charming to be around. Warm, lively, always laughing."

Bev gently guided her back. "Can you tell us what happened after you put the baby down for his nap?"

Lynda drew in a steadying breath.

"I put Tobias down around two-thirty, just as I always did. I sat with him for a bit in the nursery, waiting for him to settle. When he drifted off, I slipped out so I could put some diapers in the wash."

"How long were you out of the room?" Bev asked.

"Only a few minutes." Lynda's lip trembled and Maisie noticed her fingers twisting together again in her lap.

"He slept so soundly, and he was safe in his crib. I never imagined...I never imagined anything bad could happen." She shook her head. "So I left him there in his room and went down to the laundry. I couldn't have been gone more than five minutes."

Her face crumbled, and she took a shuddering breath.

Maisie waited for what she knew was coming.

Tears flowed freely down Lynda's face now. "But when I came back, he wasn't there."

"I'm so sorry," Maisie whispered, feeling for her.

"What did you do next?" Bev asked.

She took a moment to wipe her eyes, then gulped in a breath. "At first I thought Ada had come in and picked him up, so I went to find her. But she hadn't. And Robert didn't have him either." She pressed a trembling hand to her cheek. "I'll never forget the look on their faces when we realized he was missing." A sob escaped her. "Their baby was gone... and it felt like my fault."

"It wasn't your fault," Bev said. "You didn't do anything wrong. What happened was the kidnapper's doing. Not yours."

"Try telling that to my heart," she murmured, dabbing at her eyes.

Maisie could only imagine the guilt she must feel, even though what Bev said was true. It wasn't Lynda's fault.

"So, what do you think happened?" she asked Lynda, who'd pulled a tissue out of her pocket and was dabbing her eyes.

"I don't know. I just don't know. Someone obviously came into the house, took advantage of the fact that almost everybody was outside, and snatched Tobias."

"Pretty risky," Bev said.

"It's lucky they weren't discovered," Maisie added.

"They must have picked their moment," Lynda said, frowning. "Maybe they were even watching the house. Watching me." She shuddered and wrapped her arms around herself.

"Then what happened?" Maisie asked.

"I went to find Ada, and when I realized she didn't have Tobias, we told Robert. He arranged a manhunt. Everybody thought the kidnapper must have run off into the woods."

"You're sure they didn't drive away?"

"Only the guests' cars were at the house, and they were all accounted for."

Maisie frowned. It did seem like the woods was the most likely option.

"I know he's probably long dead," Lynda whispered. "I just hope he didn't suffer."

Neither Maisie nor Bev said anything, although after forty years and no sightings, she was probably right.

Chapter 10

Swinging By The Golf Club

The next day, Maisie took a long lunch break and set off for the Sycamore Hill Golf Estate. She gazed out of the window as she drove, marveling at the rolling green expanse of farmland sloping off into the distance and the vineyards with their neat, straight rows. With the mist clinging to the valley, it felt like she'd stumbled upon a movie set for a fantasy film. It was so different to L.A.

She went by herself, since everybody else was either busy or working. It was Bev who had arranged her meeting with June Penrose. The two knew each other from when Bev had been sheriff. Maisie wasn't sure what reason Bev had given for the interview, but she assumed it had something to do with the town's history or maybe even the tapestry itself. Either way, June had agreed and Maisie was eager to meet her.

She left the town and drove north for a mile or so. The golf estate lay on the far side of the valley, stretching across several acres. She could see the wide, manicured fairways from the interstate, cutting into the landscape. The smooth grass was broken only by bunkers, stands of conifers, and the glinting blue water of a man-made pond. Behind the course, stretching north along the ridge, was a seemingly endless expanse of Douglas firs.

Maisie turned into the golf estate and cruised up a winding drive until the peaked roof of the sprawling clubhouse came into view. It was flanked by a parking lot full of gleaming sedans and SUVs. She pulled in between a Range rover and a shiny new EV and switched off the engine.

Built from timber and stone, the building looked like a mountain lodge that had gone corporate, with grand wraparound decks, massive glass windows reflecting the sky, and a carved wooden sign out front that read *Sycamore Hill Golf Estate.*

After checking her reflection in the rear-view mirror, she stepped out of the car. As she walked to the front entrance, she heard the low murmur of conversation spilling from the restaurant terrace. A pair of golfers passed her on their way out, their spikes clicking across the path, laughing about a missed putt.

The double doors stood open, so she went inside. A receptionist stood at a desk near the door, and Maisie was about to make her way over when she heard a clipped, feminine voice behind her.

"You must be Maisie. I've been expecting you."

She turned, a ready smile on her face. "I am. It's good to meet you, Mrs. Penrose. Thank you for seeing me."

"Of course." June extended a slim hand and they shook.

Maisie saw her glance down, almost surprised, at her bracelets that jingled along with the handshake.

June Penrose was a handsome woman in her sixties with a slender physique and high cheekbones. She wore her professionally silver-streaked hair in a fashionable bob, and in her ears were understated, but clearly expensive, gold earrings.

She was stylishly dressed in beige slacks, fashionable slingbacks, and the most beautiful cream cashmere sweater. Maisie couldn't help but admire the soft, whisper-fine fibers with a four-ply twist that gave the cashmere its distinctive matte sheen.

That was not from a department store.

The outfit was finished off with a simple gold necklace. This woman had perfected the art of quiet luxury, Maisie thought, as she followed her across the lobby to her office.

"Bev suggested I talk to you since I'm trying to find out a little more about your estate," she said, hurrying to keep up with June's quick, business-like stride.

"A subject close to my heart. My office is this way. We can talk privately there."

They marched through a lounge and bar area furnished with low tables, leather seating, and a flickering gas fireplace. Maisie would have liked to sit there and talk, it was so cozy, but June led her down a carpeted corridor to an open doorway.

"I appreciate you coming a few minutes early. I have a tight schedule today," she said, gesturing for Maisie to step through.

The first thing Maisie noticed was how the office décor matched the woman's personal style. It was decorated in tones of beige, gold, maple, and cream. She sat down in one of two linen armchairs positioned in front of June's desk.

"We're welcoming a delegation of Japanese politicians today," June added, stepping around the desk to sit in her own chair instead of beside her, which would have been more casual. "Apparently they're huge golfing fans."

Since it was free, Maisie set her tote bag on the other chair. "They sound important."

June gave a curt nod. "I believe they have business in Portland. We're used to such guests, however. The governor is one of our regular VIPs, and we often get celebrities coming out to relax off the grid."

Maisie looked out of the wide windows at the green expanse beyond. The forest provided a dark backdrop to the emerald green of the fairways. "I can see why. You have a gorgeous property."

June bowed her head. "We have done a lot to it in recent years. Now, what specifically was it that you wanted to know? Bev said you might like to take some of our flyers to advertise in your store."

Maisie smiled. Crafty Bev. "I'd be happy to. But first, could you tell me a little about the history of Sycamore Hill? I read that you bought it from the Hollowells, is that right?"

June nodded matter-of-factly. "That's correct. The estate was mainly farmland back then—and forest, of course. We put a considerable amount of effort into creating the estate. It was William, my husband's, vision. He's got the Penrose ambitious streak running through his veins. You're familiar with Silas Penrose, William's grandfather, I presume? He was one of the founders of Thistle Grove."

"I am, yes. I've been learning about the town's history," Maisie said. "I heard Silas Penrose was in a partnership with Augustus Rutherford. Is that right?"

"Yes. Both men brought something to the table and together they built something great."

"It is a fascinating story, and a lovely town," Maisie said, smiling. "You must be very proud of what they accomplished."

"I am." June glanced at her wristwatch.

Maisie steered the conversation back to the real reason for her visit. The Hollowells. "Did you keep any of the existing buildings or features?" she asked idly, hoping to segway into the more serious side of the discussion.

"Oh, no," June scoffed. "There was nothing left of the main house after the fire. I'm sure you heard about that?" She arched a perfectly plucked eyebrow, and Maisie nodded.

"Did you rebuild on the site of the original structure?" she asked, knowing that they hadn't.

"Not at all. The original property was closer to the tree-line. Higher up, on the ridge. The first thing we did was clear the rubble and ashes away."

"That must have been awfully upsetting. I heard you were actually at the house when the Hollowells' baby went missing. A summer party, or something like that?"

June blinked, caught off guard by the question. "Oh. Er, yes. I was. That was a terrible day. Just terrible."

"Can you tell me about that?" Maisie asked, without giving her time to recover herself.

"Why do you want to know?" she asked, tucking a hair behind her ear.

"Like I said, I'm interested in the town's history. I'm new, and something of a true crime buff, so I thought it would be good to speak to you, since you know everybody there is to know around this area."

She gave a brief nod. "I suppose that's true." A beat passed. "That day, at the party, I was heavily pregnant at the time, and what happened shook me up. I began to feel unwell, and had to go home."

"I'm so sorry," Maisie whispered.

"My Greg was born a few days later." Her voice wavered. "To think someone could do that to a defenseless infant." She shook her head at the injustice of it.

Maisie didn't miss the slight tremor of her hands. Like Glynis and Lynda, she could tell the memory still haunted her, even after all this time.

They were interrupted by a knock on the doorframe. A middle-aged, bearded man stuck his head into the room.

"I'm sorry to interrupt, dear," he said in the same clipped voice. "Our Japanese visitors are due to arrive shortly."

"This is my husband, William," June said, sitting up straight. "William, this is Maisie Button, owner of that cute little craft store in town."

"Hello." Maisie could tell from William's polite smile that he had never heard of it. "Are you looking to join our club?"

"Not right now," Maisie said politely. "I'm just interested in our local history."

William nodded, distracted.

"Actually, we were just talking about the Hollowells' garden party," Maisie continued, hoping to hold his attention. "June was about to tell me what happened that day."

June shot her a sharp look. "I wasn't—"

"It was an awful day," William cut in, his gaze returning to Maisie's. He shook his head. "Best forgotten."

"Did you help with the search?" Maisie asked.

A somber nod. "For all the good that it did. We couldn't find the infant. It was as if he'd disappeared into thin air. God knows what became of him."

"I don't want to think about it," June murmured.

"No, of course not." He rubbed at his temples. "June, I need something for this goddamn headache. Can you get me an Advil before the Japanese arrive?"

"Yes, of course." She turned to Maisie. "If you'll excuse me."

Maisie got to her feet. "Of course. Thank you for your time. I'll see myself out."

Chapter 11

A Good Yarn

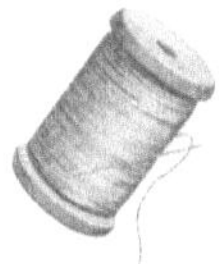

Rutherford Timber and Land Management sat quietly at the northeast edge of Thistle Grove, right where the town gave way to the endless sweep of piney woods stretching out beyond Sycamore Hill.

Maisie glanced at the digital display on her dashboard. It was just before noon, and she was right on time for her appointment with Harriet Rutherford.

After yesterday's talk with June Penrose, she'd decided that she needed to speak to the other woman who'd been there that day. Luckily, Harriet was a knitter and a fan of the store, so when Maisie had called her with her request to talk about the town's history, she'd gladly agreed.

As she pulled into the yard, she gazed through the windshield at the long, low-slung brick building that looked like it hadn't changed much since the seventies, except maybe for the fresh coat of paint and the neatly trimmed shrubs lining the front walk.

She parked beside a white pickup truck bearing the company's name and pine-tree logo in forest green. Climbing out of the car, Maisie paused and listened to the rustling of the trees behind the building, the chirping bird sounds, and the soft tinkle of a gurgling creek.

They were surrounded by trees—those same woods that stretched on for miles. It was so refreshing.

Harriet met her in the lobby. "Maisie! It's good to see you."

Unlike June Penrose, Harriet was a practical dresser, and despite being in her mid-sixties, wore sturdy jeans, a flannel shirt and a fleece vest with the Rutherford Timber and Land Management logo stitched over the heart.

Her hair was pulled back in a messy bun, with rebellious tendrils curling around her ears. There was a healthy flush on her ruddy cheeks, and she had sharp, intelligent eyes the color of sage.

Behind her, the lobby hummed with activity. A young man at the reception desk juggled phone calls with practiced ease, while employees moved purposefully through the space, some balancing coffee cups, others carrying stacks of paperwork, all with an efficient, unhurried air.

"Busy day?" Maisie fell into step beside her as they started down a wide hallway lined with framed aerial photos of the surrounding woodlands.

"You know how it is," Harriet replied over her shoulder with a little chuckle. "Spring always stirs things up. Permits, inspections, land use meetings—and that's before we even get to the fun part. Boundary disputes."

Maisie laughed. She'd always liked Harriet. There was nothing pretentious or superficial about her. Just a genuinely nice person, despite her wealth and pedigree.

"Do you know much about our company?" Harriet asked as they turned into a large conference room.

"Very little," Maisie admitted with a sheepish smile. "Wow, look at that view!"

All thoughts of history flew from her head as she stared out of the floor-to-ceiling windows that framed the forest like a painting.

The trees stood tall and quiet just beyond the glass, their dark green needles glistening in the dappled sunlight. Above, the cloudless blue sky cast a cheery light over everything, bringing the greens and browns of the Douglas firs to life.

"This is my favorite room in the whole building," Harriet said, grinning. "That's why I brought you here."

"It's exquisite. I'd be so distracted if I had to have meetings here. I'd never get anything done."

She laughed. "We are very lucky to have this as our backdrop."

They took seats at a large oval table in the center of the room. There was no need for any other décor, since it would have been dwarfed by the show nature was putting on just beyond the glass.

Maisie forced her thoughts back to the reason for her visit. "I know your company has something to do with forestry and land management. I also learned that your ancestor, Augustus Rutherford, co-founded Thistle Grove with Silas Penrose. Father Tom told me that he donated the land."

Harriet settled back in her chair, resting her elbows

comfortably on the table. "That's right. We manage most of the land Thistle Grove sits on, as well as the surrounding area."

"That's a lot of land," Maisie murmured, her gaze drifting back to the window.

"It is," Harriet agreed with a small nod. "Augustus Rutherford arrived in Oregon during a time when land was being offered up to settlers and developers. He struck a deal when he proposed founding Thistle Grove with Silas Penrose. The government let him keep the whole parcel instead of splitting it off. So, he created Rutherford Timber to manage the land—and that's what we still do today."

She followed Maisie's gaze. "We oversee the land for all sorts of uses. Recreational trails, timber harvesting, livestock grazing, even some environmental research."

Maisie tilted her head. "And your family still owns all of that?"

Harriet nodded. "All except for what's been sold to the church, homeowners and businesses within the town limits. We also maintain about a thousand hectares of forest that we harvest for timber, although we do it sustainably. Beyond our boundaries, it's mostly federal land."

"Are your daughters planning to take over eventually?" Maisie asked. "I remember you mentioning you had two girls."

"I do, and I certainly hope so," Harriet said, a note of fondness in her voice. "They're both off at college right now. One is studying law, the other finance. The idea is they'll come back and take over someday, but we'll see. Frank and I are trying not to pressure them. You have to let kids find their own path, you know?"

Maisie nodded. She didn't have kids but that sounded

like good parenting. "I spoke to someone at town hall who mentioned that you hold a lot of the town's land records?"

"Oh yes," Harriet said, sitting up a bit straighter. "We've got everything from original deeds to zoning maps. What are you looking for?"

She thought about what Father Tom had said. "Do you have the original land sale documents for St. Paul's Episcopal Church?"

"Remind me to print you out a copy before you leave. We have that on file as a matter of record."

"That would be great." Maisie paused. "Also, I've been digging into the history of Sycamore Hill..."

"Oh, I know that property well." Harriet gave a knowing smile. "The Hollowell family owned it back in the early eighties, and then the Penroses bought it to build the golf estate. If you want records going back more than fifty years, I'd need to dig into the archives."

"That's okay," Maisie said, then hesitated. "What I'm curious about is the Hollowell family tragedy. Someone told me you and Frank were at the party when baby Tobias went missing?"

Harriet's smile faltered. "Why do you want to know about that?"

Same question as June Penrose had asked. Maisie gave her the same answer. "Just curious, I guess. We were talking about it in my Knit and Natter group the other night. Plus, I'm something of a cold case enthusiast."

"Both of my daughters are hooked on those podcasts," she said with a grimace.

"Would you mind telling me what you remember from that day?"

Harriet shifted in her chair. "Sure. I don't mind talking

about it. Though I'll warn you, it's a hard subject for some folks in town. The baby disappearing was bad enough, but then the fire and Ada's death..." She shook her head. "It left a mark on this place. People were never quite the same after that."

Maisie absorbed Harriet's words. "You and Frank were both there that day? At the summer party?"

Harriet's eyes glazed as she thought back. "I'd forgotten about that. It really was a fabulous party. Ada and Robert went all out. Everything set up on the lawn, the tables under those big canvas canopies, string lights in the trees. So Hollywood. And the weather couldn't have been more perfect. I remember there wasn't a cloud in the sky."

She paused, glancing back at Maisie. "Their property was beautiful back then. Pure farmland, untouched and wide open. Have you been out to Sycamore Hill?"

"I went yesterday," Maisie said.

Harriet nodded. "There weren't any manicured lawns back then, of course. The mansion sat right up near the tree-line, overlooking the slope of the land below. From the front porch, you could see for miles. That's part of why everyone assumed the kidnapper had come from the woods. There was nothing behind the house but dense forest. Not even an access road."

"What about neighbors?" Maisie asked.

Harriet shook her head. "Nothing but trees."

Maisie leaned forward. "When did you first realize something was wrong?"

"I'm not sure." Harriet scratched her head. "I think it was twenty minutes or so after Ada had shown her baby to us. He really was the cutest little thing. Bright blue eyes and chubby little cheeks." Her voice trailed off.

"I know it's hard," Maisie said, giving her an encouraging nod.

"Well, we heard a commotion," she said, taking a breath. "The nanny was screaming that Tobias was missing. Ada seemed shell shocked, then started crying. Everyone was stunned."

"Did the nanny say what had happened?" Maisie asked.

"Yes, apparently she'd gone to check on him and he'd vanished."

Maisie could imagine the scene. Guests in linen dresses and suits milling around with glasses of lemonade, making small talk in the bright summer sunshine. Then, the realization that something was terribly wrong.

"The whole event turned into a giant search party," Harriet went on. "People scattered across the property, checking the house, the garden. A group of the men—Frank included—headed into the woods. It was chaos."

"Was the sheriff's department called right away?" Maisie asked.

"Oh yes." Harriet nodded. "Robert called them right away. By the time they arrived, we'd already split into smaller groups to search, but we didn't find anything."

"Nothing at all?" Maisie enquired. "No footprints, no sign of a struggle or an intruder?"

"Nothing at all," Harriet whispered. "It was like the poor thing had vanished into thin air."

That was also what June had said.

"Very traumatic," Maisie sympathized. "For all concerned."

"It was," Harriet agreed, more tendrils sneaking loose. "Although I was younger back then. Still a year away from starting a family, so I didn't really appreciate the severity of it. It felt... surreal."

Maisie nodded, that made sense.

"Now, of course, as a mother—I can't even bring myself to think too long about it." She screwed up her face, closing her eyes. "That kind of loss, that not-knowing... it must have been devastating."

Maisie gave her a moment to compose her thoughts. She could only imagine how devastating.

"What do *you* think really happened?" she said, after a long beat.

A quiet sigh. "I truly don't know. After the disappearance, the rumors started. Some of them were awful. People whispering that Ada had harmed him, or that Robert had enemies. None of it made any sense to me. Ada was devoted to that child. You could see it, even just watching her with him at the party."

That was the general consensus, although some people, like the mayor, obviously disagreed.

Maisie tilted her head. "Did anyone seem overly interested in the baby? Hovering a bit too long, maybe?"

Harriet thought for a moment. "Not that I noticed, but then I wasn't looking for that. As far as I can recall, we went over for a quick peek, cooed a bit and moved on. It wasn't a mumsy type of crowd. Too many Hollywood starlets, you know?"

Maisie nodded.

"I really wish I had seen something. Maybe I could have helped, but I didn't."

"I'm sorry," Maisie whispered. That one tragedy had affected so many people. Even forty years later, the effects still lingered.

For a moment, they sat in silence, watching the dappled sunlight dance over the forest scene outside.

Then Harriet said, "But you know what strikes me, all these years later?"

Maisie looked at her expectantly.

"Whoever took that baby, they knew what they were doing. To get it out of the house like that, off the property without anyone seeing a thing. It must have been planned way in advance."

Maisie gave a slow nod. She didn't disagree.

Chapter 12

Fiery Indignation

It was midafternoon when Maisie got back to the store. Wispy clouds had encroached on the blue, and a stiff breeze had picked up, blowing her hair around her face, and causing the fairy lights in Main Street to creak on their thin cables.

Unlocking the door, she flipped the sign back to *Open*, and glanced around for Mewsly, but the tabby didn't appear to be home.

Taking advantage of the quiet, she unfolded the printout Harriet had given her. On it was a map that outlined the area of land purchased by the church.

Maisie remembered Father Tom telling her that the land had been acquired through a deal brokered by Augustus Rutherford and Silas Penrose on behalf of the church leaders. Silas had then further donated capital in order to construct the church.

She studied the sale deed, which contained three signatures. Augustus, Silas and an unknown church official. Maisie guessed this would be similar to what Father Tom would give them once he'd dug out the church records.

A knock on the front door made her turn around. Outside stood a man with two overflowing bundles of flowers where his head should be. Behind him, a charcoal-gray pickup was parked haphazardly along the curb.

She jumped up and opened the door. "Jesse, come on in."

Jesse Morland was an easygoing young man in his twenties. He had messy brown hair and warm hazel eyes and worked at the local garden center.

"Hi Maisie. Your weekly flower delivery," he announced, looking around.

"Put them down on the table," she said, hastily picking up the printout and folding it up. "I'll get a couple of vases."

He did so, and Maisie brough back two hobnail milk glass vases that she'd half-filled with water.

"Oh, they're beautiful!" The arrangements were bursting with soft, dusky purples and vivid blues, balanced by tiny periwinkles, creamy whites, and sprigs of wild greenery that gave them a perfectly untamed look. "I didn't think your aunt could top last week's, but these are absolutely stunning."

"You lit a fire in her," Jesse said, grinning as he peeled off the paper wrapper. "Ever since you said you liked the wildflower look, she's been calling every supplier in the region. She said she hasn't had this much fun in years."

Maisie laughed. "Well, I'm glad I could bring out her inner artist."

Jesse glanced around the store. "Having a good day?"

"Yes, thanks." Maisie slipped the blooms into the vases. "How about you? Still juggling two jobs?"

Jesse stretched his neck. "Yep. Garden center's always hopping this time of year with the spring planting, and the golf estate's got a landscaping project going on, so I've been back and forth between the two."

Maisie shot him a sympathetic smile. He worked at Sycamore Hill too, helping out the head gardener there. With all those fairways she'd seen the other day, she was surprised he had any time at all to dedicate to the garden center.

Then again, Jesse was dependable to a fault. She knew all about his history from the Knit and Natter ladies. This was a small town, after all. Not much was sacred.

From what she'd heard, Jesse's mom had passed away when he was little, and his father had run off, not wanting to take on the responsibility of being a single dad. So he'd been raised by his aunt and uncle, both of whom were long time residents of Thistle Grove.

The bell above the door jingled and in swept MJ wearing a daffodil-yellow sundress that clashed wonderfully with her scuffed army boots.

"Hey," she called, lifting her chin and sniffing the air. "Smells amazing in here. Did the flower fairy pay a visit?"

Jesse straightened at the sound of her voice and hastily ran a hand through his hair.

"He's still here," Maisie supplied, smiling.

MJ came over and admired the bouquets. "Nice work."

Jesse beamed. "All my aunt's doing, really. I'm just the delivery guy."

Maisie glanced between the two of them.

"Why don't you stay for coffee?" she asked Jesse. "MJ was just about to put on a fresh pot."

MJ blinked. "I was?"

"If you wouldn't mind?" Maisie asked, smiling sweetly.

"Okay."

MJ wandered over to the machine, oblivious of Jesse's eyes on her.

"Jesse?" Maisie prompted.

The youngster hesitated, but only for a moment. "Sure. Why not?"

"Great."

As MJ put the machine on, Maisie went to the back and unwrapped a tray of cookies. Last night's attempt at a new recipe.

"Not sure what these are like," she said, putting the plate down on the table next to the flowers. "You can be my guinea pig."

Jessie chuckled and reached for one. "Thanks."

"Don't eat them all," MJ called. "They're for tonight's meeting."

"Meeting?" He paused, cookie suspended in the air.

"Go ahead, you're allowed one," Maisie said. "It's only our knitting circle."

"I thought that was Friday?"

"It is, but since Margot died, we've been meeting more regularly," MJ said, then glanced at Maisie and cringed. "Sorry."

"But Jesse didn't think anything of it. His smile faded, though.

"I heard about that and I'm sorry for your loss."

"Thank you."

MJ returned with the pot and a tray of mugs. She set about pouring the coffee.

Jesse glanced at the bouquets Maisie had put into the vases.

"Want me to arrange these for you? My aunt's been teaching me a few tricks."

"Sure," Maisie said warmly. "Go right ahead. I've got to unpack some boxes, so I'll be right back."

"I'll help you," MJ said, and Maisie saw Jesse's face fall.

"That's okay. You guys chat. I won't be long."

Before MJ had a chance to object, she left them at the table and went to the storeroom at the back.

She was rummaging through boxes when she heard the front door open. Poking her head out, she saw Mayor Penrose had stridden into the store. An unfazed Mewsly sauntered in behind him.

"Maisie!" called MJ, from the table where she was sorted a pile of odd buttons.

"Mr. Mayor," Maisie stepped forward to greet him. "I didn't know you were a fan of buttons and bobbins. Can I get you a cup of coffee? It's freshly brewed."

As usual, his suit was beautifully cut—Armani or something similar—but it was a shade too formal for a Tuesday afternoon visit to a craft store.

Then again, politicians, like celebrities, dressed for cameras. Greg Penrose wanted to be taken seriously, and he wanted her, and everybody else, to see that they were speaking to someone important.

"No, but thank you." He scanned the shop like he was checking for paparazzi. "I just thought I'd stop in to check on the tapestry."

"Of course. Right this way."

She led him to the rear of the store. The tapestry, still stretched across its frame, occupied nearly the entire back space.

The mayor studied the tapestry in silence for a moment, hands behind his back. He pointed to the fire with the figure in the middle. "Why is that still there? I thought I asked you to remove it."

"It's a lot more complicated than it looks," Maisie said. "For a start, I'd have to unweave all the thread to get back to that point. If I do that, it won't be ready for the anniversary."

His jaw tightened. "It will have to be altered afterwards, then."

"It's Margot's vision," Maisie said carefully. If he wanted it redone after the anniversary, there was nothing she could do to stop him, but for now, it was staying. "I'm trying to understand what she meant by it."

"To dig up old memories? Who knows? It doesn't matter, though. It just needs to be completed for the celebration."

Maisie knew he was up for reelection. This anniversary was important to him.

He fixed his gaze on her. "You are going to be able to finish it, aren't you?"

"I'm not an expert, but I have a basic grasp of weaving. Margot has done most of the hard work. I just need to fill in the background on the last panel and make whatever changes I see fit. So yes, I think we can do it."

The Mayor grunted. "Thank you. It's good to know it's in safe hands."

In the background, she heard Jesse say something and MJ burst out laughing.

They walked back to the front of the store.

Mayor Penrose, who'd regained his composure, shot her a polite smile. "Thank you again for stepping in. Let me know when it's ready."

She nodded. "I'll be in touch."

With a creak from his shoes, he stepped out into the wind and walked away, his blazer billowing out behind him.

"I think he likes you," Maisie said, a short while later, when Jesse had left.

MJ blinked. "Who? Jesse?"

Maisie gave an enthusiastic nod.

MJ frowned. "Really? That's weird. I mean, he's so not my type."

"You seem to get on."

"That's here, but we have nothing in common."

Maisie raised an eyebrow. "How do you know?"

She rolled her eyes. "We went to the same high school, but we weren't friends. Different groups."

Maisie shook her head. "So? That was back then. This is now."

MJ tilted her head. "Okay, sure. He's cute, but he's also always so serious. All he does is work. I know it sounds mean, but he's kind of boring."

Maisie scoffed. "He's responsible. That's not the same thing as boring. It's a trait to be admired."

MJ shrugged.

Maisie pursed her lips. "I'm not saying you have to date the guy, but don't knock him for having a good work ethic."

MJ smirked. "I already have a mom, you know. And she's very vocal about who I should be dating."

Maisie raised both hands in surrender. "I would never. I'm just saying, sometimes, people surprise you. You should give him a chance."

MJ narrowed her eyes. "Are you talking from experience?"

Maisie chuckled, instinctively touching the ring on her right hand. She hadn't shared much about Frank. It was still too raw, too painful. But her friends new she'd come here for a fresh start after her husband had died. That was enough, for now.

"Kind of."

MJ nudged her. "Maybe you'll tell us about him some day."

Maisie gave a sad smile. "Maybe."

Chapter 13

A Wrongful Deed

The Knit and Natter crew trickled in just after closing. Ree was first, smoothing down her flyaway hair, while Bev marched in pink-cheeked from the wind. Cherry followed, Eloise holding a paperback novel, right behind her.

"Where's Brian?" asked MJ, who was still at her perch at the table. She'd spent the afternoon embroidering an elaborate design on a pair of old jeans.

"He's here," came Brian's booming voice as he stepped inside bringing a gust of wind with him. "I nearly got blown away on the way."

"It has picked up," Ree complained, cleaning her glasses. "But the weather is so iffy this time of year."

Maisie smiled at her choice of words and turned on the coffee maker. The machine sputtered to life with its usual clunk and hiss. Soon the aroma of ground coffee beans and hazelnuts filled the store.

"I've got some good news," Brian announced, flopping down in his usual seat at the table.

"Did Lucy and Ethel finally get chosen as the official spokes-dogs for that organic dog food brand?" Bev asked, raising an eyebrow.

Brian's dachshunds were small, long, and packed with more personality than most people's entire extended families. Maisie knew that they'd recently been front-runners in a regional "Face of Furever Fresh" contest.

According to his many Knit and Natter updates, the competition had been fierce. Top contenders had been a Sheltie with championship bloodlines and a rescue mutt with a crooked smile and a talent for walking on its hind legs.

Brian beamed as he peeled off his tweed jacket. "Nope. We're still waiting to hear about that, but this is even better."

"Does it have to do with the case?" Bev asked, eyes sparkling.

Coffee was poured—lemonade for Eloise—and the little group gathered around the table. Eloise sauntered over to the rocking chair with her book, but Mewsly, now perched on the rug, was too busy licking her left paw to take notice.

With an almost magician-like flourish, Brian reached into his leather satchel and pulled out a manila folder. He placed it on the table, then reached back in and took out a stapled stack of photocopies.

"First, I got those documents you asked for from Father Tom," he told Maisie. He spread them out over the table. Maisie recognized a sales deed similar to the one Harriet had given her.

She picked it up and inspected it. It was a report detailing the transfer of the specific church plot. Beneath it was the size of the plot, and the amount they'd paid for it.

She frowned. "Wait—"

"What's up?" MJ asked.

"I'm not sure." Maisie dug in her purse for the Rutherford Timber document and pulled it out. Comparing them side by side, she said, "I think there's a discrepancy in the figures."

Brian leaned in, scanning the two reports. His brows closed in a frown. "You're right. The church document says they paid substantially less for the land than what Rutherford Timber reports selling it for."

"Aren't they're supposed to be the same document?" MJ said, gaze narrowing.

Maisie gnawed on her lip. "Yes, they are."

"What does it mean?" asked Cherry, glancing between them.

"It's either a genuine mistake," replied Brian slowly. "Or one of the deeds is fraudulent. The church recorded something different than what Rutherford Timber has on file."

Ree gasped and put her hand over her mouth.

"Fraudulent?" whispered Cherry, her eyes wide.

Maisie frowned. "Do you think Silas Penrose and the church undercut the Rutherfords?"

Brian gave a pensive shrug. "I don't know, but something doesn't add up."

MJ snapped her fingers. "That could be what the inverted cross on the tapestry means."

Bev nodded. "Margot could have discovered the discrepancy and that's how she chose to portray it."

"Like she was leaving us a clue," Eloise added from the rocking chair.

Maisie's mind raced. Was it possible? Had they just stumbled upon a major clue? "You could be right."

"If the church was corrupt, Father Tom would be desperate not to let that get out," Bev extrapolated, pursing her lips.

"Especially now. Right before the town's 150-year anniversary celebration," Brian added.

"Desperate enough to kill over?" MJ whispered.

"No," Ree said, shaking her head. "Not Father Tom."

Bev shrugged. "It's definitely motive."

"I can't believe it." Ree kept shaking her head, refusing to acknowledge that Father Tom had been involved in Margot's murder.

Maisie had to admit, it seemed a stretch for a man of the cloth.

"We need to speak to him again," she said, finally. "We need clarity on this. Or, we take both these documents to Harriet Rutherford for her opinion."

"The second one," Cherry said.

MJ nodded.

"There's something else," Brian said, picking up the stack of papers and handing them around.

Maisie glanced down at hers. "What is this?"

"I stopped by the library and combed through the microforms collection. I was looking for anything reported around the time Tobias went missing."

"Microforms?" Cherry squinted at the sheet. "Is that like microfiche?"

"Microforms is the plural, Mom," Eloise chimed in from the floor, where she'd abandoned the chair to sit cross-legged next to Mewsly. The cat had now moved on to grooming her right paw with slow, deliberate precision. "Microfiche is just one format."

Cherry shook her head at her daughter. "You never cease to amaze me, kiddo."

Maisie scanned the photocopy in her hands. It was an article from the *Thistle Grove Crier*, the same paper that still landed, ink-smudged and slightly damp, on porches around town every Friday morning.

The headline read: *HOLLYWOOD BABY KIDNAPPED*

"It was one of the first articles published after the incident," Brian explained, sitting down again. "Probably within a day or two of the party."

Bev lifted her glasses on top of her head and looked across at him. "There's nothing new here. It ends with the usual plea from the authorities for information."

Brian shot her a knowing grin. "Ah, but look again."

They all leaned forward.

"What are we looking at?" Maisie frowned, impatient to see what he had noticed.

"The photograph," he hinted.

She studied the grainy, black-and-white photo printed in the middle of the page. A moment frozen in time. Sunlight filtering through trees while smiling guests in sunglasses gathered on the perfectly manicured lawn. At the front, in the center, stood a young woman cradling a baby in a ruffled sunhat.

"It must have been taken at the start of the party," Ree murmured. "When Lynda brought the baby out to meet everyone."

Cherry nodded. "I'm guessing the woman in the middle is Ada Hollowell and that dashing man is her husband, Robert."

Ada and Robert Hollowell were the picture of early eighties wealth and glamor. Ada was slim and elegant, with big, feathered waves and large, wide-set eyes. She was wearing a short-sleeved, A-line dress that hung just below the knee in a light, summery floral pattern. She looked slight but strong, with a happy smile.

Robert stood beside her, his arm around her waist. He was a few inches taller with dark, wavy hair, and he wore white slacks and a boldly patterned button-up shirt. They stood out even from the rest of the well-dressed partygoers.

Maisie had seen it before on film sets where she'd worked. Some people just had that X-factor. Ada radiated an unmistakable star quality even from a photocopied printout of a microfiche.

Standing next to the couple was a young woman with her hand resting on the handle of a big, old-fashioned stroller. Although she was forty years younger, Maisie immediately recognized Lynda. She also recognized younger versions of Harriet and Frank Rutherford, as well as June and William Penrose. June was standing with a hand on her rounded belly.

"What's this lead you're talking about, Brian?" Ree demanded. "From what I can tell, it looks like the photo confirms what we know already. Is there something I'm not seeing?"

Brian leaned forward and pointed to the top of the photograph.

"There's someone else in the picture, and I don't think they were invited."

Maisie squinted at the photograph. "It's too grainy to see clearly. Does anyone have a magnifying glass?"

Ree reached into her knitting tote without missing a beat. "Always. Comes in handy for crossword clues."

Maisie leaned over the photo with the magnifier.

Then she saw it—and gasped.

A man stood at the back, tucked amongst the trees. Watching.

She blinked, and looked again, but all she could make out were the vague contours of his face. Tall, physically well-built, but with blurred features.

MJ noticed him too. "There's a man! Behind everyone, in the trees."

"Who is that?" Cherry held the page up to her nose. "I can't make him out."

Brian flipped open his notebook with a flourish. "His name is Jed Sutter. According to another article I found, the sheriff didn't even know he'd been there until this photo ran in the *Crier*. It was an eagle-eyed reader who spotted him and called it in."

He unfolded an old article and lay it on the table. This headline read: *MOUNTAIN MAN QUESTIONED*.

Bev snorted. "Mountain Man? Seriously?"

"He lived out in the woods," Maisie said, scanning the article. "A recluse, apparently."

Brian gave a firm nod. "Exactly. Would anyone like me to read this one aloud?"

"Er, yeah," Eloise said from the floor, echoing what everyone else was thinking.

Brian cleared his throat and began. "*Local recluse Jed Sutter has been interviewed by Thistle Grove's Sheriff Wyden under suspicion of involvement in the recent kidnapping of Tobias Hollowell who vanished from under his parents' nose during a boozy garden party.*"

Cherry let out a huff. "Boozy! They make it sound like it's the parents' fault the baby was taken."

Brian continued. "*The authorities were made aware of the suspect after sharp-eyed Crier readers spotted Sutter in the background of a photograph published in our last edition.*"

Now the Hollowells' groundskeeper has come forward to claim he saw a shadowy figure in the trees around the time of the child's disappearance."

"Groundskeeper?" Bev perked up. "That might be someone we can talk to."

"Unfortunately not." Brian winced. "I already looked him up. He passed away twelve years ago."

"Pity." Ree shook her head. "Would've been good to hear what he had to say."

Brian resumed reading. *"Thistle Grove residents with knowledge of Sutter describe him as a loner with little social contact.* And here's a quote from one of the store owners: *'I see him in town once a week, picking up supplies. Doesn't talk much. I don't know much about him. Nobody does.'"*

He raised his eyebrows as he turned the page. *"Law enforcement officers searched Jed Sutter's remote cabin but found no trace of the missing child, nor any evidence linking him to the crime. He was found to be in legal possession of a shotgun, which he claims he uses for hunting.*

"Wyden wasn't much better than Markham," Bev muttered. "I believe he didn't last long."

"This case probably killed his career," Maisie mused.

Brian held up a finger. "Here's a quote from a local resident. *'Jed Sutter is a loner and lives out in the woods. Who knows what he gets up to out there?'"*

"She's casting aspersions," MJ muttered.

"How old was Sutter back then?" Ree asked, pushing her glasses up her nose.

"Mid-thirties," Maisie replied, eyes still on the article. "He'd be in his seventies now."

"My age," Ree said, thoughtful. "I wonder if he's still around. I could ask people at the senior center. Somebody might know him."

"Good idea." Cherry nodded in agreement. "He sounds like a solid lead."

MJ tapped the corner of the photo. "It can't be a coincidence, can it? He's literally hanging out in the trees watching the party, right before the baby disappears."

Maisie shuddered. It did sound ominous, but they had to keep an open mind. "Maybe he was just curious. We know he was a loner, and he didn't have much social interaction. Just because he was watching, doesn't mean he was involved."

Brian shot her a skeptical look. "You're kidding, right? This is a solid lead."

Cherry folded her arms. "Maisie, there's seeing the good in people, and then there's completely ignoring what's right in front of your nose. Creeping out of the woods, staring at a party full of strangers? That's weird."

"He was cleared by the sheriff," Maisie said calmly. "They would've found something if he'd taken the baby."

"Not necessarily," Brian said. "He might have... disposed of it by then."

Ree crinkled her nose. "I don't want to think about that."

MJ narrowed her gaze, still fixed on the photograph.

"What are you thinking, Bev?" Maisie asked the former sheriff, who was staring into her coffee cup.

"I think it's worth finding him," Bev replied, meeting her gaze. "Even if he didn't take the infant, he might have seen or heard something useful."

"You mean like the kidnapper?" Maisie asked.

Bev nodded. "Given his background, he may not have felt comfortable talking to the sheriff or his deputies. Some loners are like that. They don't trust law enforcement."

MJ looked doubtful. "How exactly are we going to find

him? He's a hermit who lives in the middle of nowhere. Even if we did locate him, I doubt he wants a knitting circle knocking on his cabin door."

"True," Bev admitted. "But just because he lives out in the sticks, doesn't mean he's dangerous."

"He has a shotgun," Ree pointed out.

Bev shrugged. "You'd have to, living out there alone."

Maisie shifted in her chair. "If this guy, Sutter, did see something, why would he open up now?"

Cherry crossed her arms. "Exactly. He's in his seventies. All the more reason to keep quiet."

Bev sighed. "Time has a way of changing a person. They soften, they have regrets, they get tired of carrying secrets. If Jed Sutter knows anything about what happened that day, he might finally be ready to tell someone."

The room went quiet for a beat, the only sound the faint purring of Mewsly as she curled up in Eloise's lap, at last satisfied with the state of her paws.

Maisie gave a reluctant nod. "Let's hope you're right."

Chapter 14

The Power Of Glazed Donuts

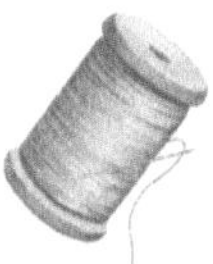

It was Ree who managed to track down Jed Sutter.

A friend of a friend who played bingo with Ree every Wednesday night at the senior center, knew Jed Sutter's cousin, Irma. So it was armed with that information, and a box of glazed donuts from Dillard's Bakehouse, that Ree paid Irma a visit.

"It turned out to be a very interesting discussion," Ree told the group that evening. "Jed is a recluse, but he's not off the grid. She gave me directions to his cabin."

"She did?" Maisie asked. "Wow. I didn't think it would be that easy."

"Never underestimate the power of glazed donuts," Ree said, seriously.

Maisie laughed.

"Do you know how to get there?" Cherry asked.

"Well, he doesn't have an actual address," Ree explained. "But once a month, Irma drives out to meet him and drop off supplies. There's an access road that takes you half the way there. The rest is on foot."

"She goes on foot with boxes of supplies?" MJ said. "Isn't she your age?"

Ree chuckled. "Jed meets her at the end of the access road."

MJ exhaled.

"Why does he live out there?" Eloise asked, from the rocking chair.

Ree shrugged. "She didn't say, but I could tell she worries about him out there all by himself."

"Aren't there bears and stuff?" Eloise asked.

"I'm sure there are," Bev said with a nod.

MJ shivered. "I would be way too scared to stay somewhere that isolated."

"Me too," Maisie concurred. After L.A. Thistle Grove felt like the countryside.

"So, how are we going to talk to him?" Bev asked. "I'm not hiking out there. My knees couldn't handle it."

"Don't look at me," Ree said. "I'd never make it past the trailhead."

"I'm out as well," Brian said apologetically. "Our other librarian's down with the flu, and someone's got to keep the circulation desk from catching fire in her absence."

Maisie set down her mug.

"I'll do it," she said simply. "I'm not afraid to talk to him. I really don't think a seventy-year-old man is much of a threat. I'll go tomorrow. It's Sunday and my only day off."

"You can't go on your own," MJ said, horrified. "I'd come but I have to work." She had a part-time job at a local diner and Sunday was one of their busiest days.

"I'll come with you," Cherry announced.

"Isn't it dangerous, mom?" Eloise said, glancing up from her novel.

"No, of course not, kiddo. It's a hike. We've done lots of those."

She frowned but went back to her book.

"I'll have to find a sitter, of course," she said, glancing around the group.

"That I can help with," Ree said, smiling at Eloise.

"Great, thank you." Cherry looked at Maisie. "So, we all set?"

Maisie grinned. "I guess so."

That evening, after the shop closed and the last customer had left, Maisie called Harriet Rutherford.

"I was wondering if you'd had a chance to look over those two deeds I sent you?"

A beat passed, before Harriet replied.

"I did, and I showed them to my husband. To be honest, we're both confused by the discrepancy. My family's records clearly show the price of the sale to be substantially more than what was recorded by the church. I can only assume there was an error on the church's side. It's unlikely Augustus Rutherford would have incorrectly recorded the sale. He was a stickler for detail."

"That's what I thought." Maise pursed her lips thoughtfully. Had the church really made a mistake, or had they paid the lower price? In which case, it was possible Augustus had been undercut without realizing it.

"Do you have any bank records from back then that would show the sale amount?" Maisie asked. It was a long shot, but you never knew. They may have accounting records going that far back.

"I can look, but I very much doubt it. We only archived the most important documents from back then. But I will take a look and let you know."

"I'd appreciate it," Maisie said.

"Was there anything else?" Harriet asked, sounding weary. The discrepancy would be playing on her mind.

"Actually, yes. Do you have a map of the forest region? The part your family owns—with the old service road marked?"

"Of course. Do you mind if I ask why you want it?"

"We're thinking about doing a nature walk," Maisie said, ignoring the twinge of guilt. It wasn't a lie. Not really. She just hadn't divulged the destination. Part of the reason was that she wasn't sure how Harriet would feel about them hiking into the middle of the forest to find a cabin in the woods.

Luckily, Harriet didn't question it.

"Sure, I'll email it to you. Enjoy the birdsong. It's wonderful this time of year."

First thing Sunday morning, Maisie and Cherry prepared to set out to track down Jed Sutter. They had filled their water bottles, packed extra layers, and stuffed their backpack with snacks, a first aid kit, and a folded trail map. Cherry had added a pair of worn hiking boots to the back, just in case the path turned muddy.

Mewsly had been fed and given fresh water, then let out for her usual morning prowl around the neighborhood. Maisie planned to be home well before supper.

Cherry had already dropped Eloise off at Ree's house. "I left them drinking hot chocolate and playing board games," she'd said as Maisie climbed into the passenger's seat and buckled up.

"Then let's go!" Maisie said, as Cherry started her SUV's engine.

They drove through the quiet Sunday morning streets of Thistle Grove, past neat rows of houses and the bakery just setting out its first trays for the day. A few early risers walked their dogs or waved as the SUV passed. Before long, the last of the town slipped behind them, and the road stretched ahead, bordered by fields and patches of trees that grew thicker with each mile.

As they approached the Rutherford land, the forest seemed to close in around them.

The map from Harriet rested between the seats, annotated in Maisie's handwriting and highlighted for good measure.

"I brought matches, flares, and a first aid kit," Cherry said, her eyes on the road as it curved amid the pines. "You know. Just in case."

Maisie glanced across at her. "Let's hope we don't need them."

Cherry scoffed. "I'm a mom. I carry Band-Aids everywhere."

Eventually, the old service road ended in a gravel turn-around, ringed by brambles and tall grass. Cherry turned the SUV to face the direction they'd come, then cut the engine. "In case we needed to make a quick getaway."

Maisie stared at her. "You're starting to scare me."

Once out of the car, they pulled on their backpacks and studied the map.

"We're headed *here*." Maisie pointed to a pen-marked spot just off-center.

Cherry fished a compass out of her coat pocket. "According to that, we walk in a north-east direction."

Maisie tilted her head to consult the compass. "Which is that way."

"Yep," Cherry agreed.

They set off. Soon the ground opened up into a kind of worn pathway.

"Looks like a trail," Cherry said, nodding to the ground. "We can follow this. The compass will keep us on a north-east heading."

"I'm so glad you came with me," Maisie admitted with a laugh. "I don't know what I was thinking attempting this alone."

"You can take the girl out of L.A." she quipped.

Maisie rolled her eyes. "I know." She glanced back over her shoulder as the trail head disappeared from view. "That must be where Irma meets Jed."

Cherry nodded. "He must be pretty fit to hike up here once a month."

They followed the curling trail between mossy roots and low-hanging branches until it veered to the south. "We have to continue this way," Cherry pointed out, glancing at the compass.

"If a seventy-year-old man can do it, so can we," Maisie muttered, as she followed Cherry into the brush.

At first, the terrain was easy, with flat stretches of ground softened by a thick layer of pine needles. The air carried a clean, crisp scent of cedar and damp earth. Birds called to one another high in the trees, and sunlight filtered through the branches, falling in soft patches along the path.

After an hour or so, however, the ground began to slope upwards. Maisie's thighs started to ache.

"Shouldn't have stopped going to the gym," she complained. "My cardio's terrible."

"Come on. It's just a brisk stroll," Cherry said.

"It's all right for you, roller derby queen," Maisie muttered.

Cherry laughed. "You have to admit it's beautiful."

Maisie couldn't deny that. The trees stood tall and close together, their trunks straight and steady, the forest floor thick with needles and fallen leaves. Ferns spread out along the edges of the trail, and the air felt cooler here, shaded from the sun. Somewhere nearby, water moved over rocks in a steady, quiet rush. The path curved ahead, disappearing into the trees, calm and undisturbed.

There was a flash of brown as a black-tailed deer darted into the trees ahead of them.

"Did you see that!" Maisie whispered.

Cherry followed her gaze just in time to see it disappear into the brush. "El is going to love hearing about this. I wish I'd gotten a photograph."

"There might be more," Maisie said.

"Maybe we'll spot a cougar, or a bear."

Maisie gulped. "No thanks. I'm good with bunnies, or maybe a fox."

Cherry snorted.

They stepped onto a line of slick stones to cross a shallow stream, Maisie wobbling as her boot slipped and nearly splashing into the water. By the time she found her balance, they were both laughing, and it felt like a good place to stop for lunch. A sturdy fallen log just off the trail, close enough to keep their bearings, made a convenient bench. They sat down and pulled out their trail snacks.

"We're two hours in," Cherry said, consulting her watch.

"Are we still headed in the right direction?" Maisie asked.

"Yeah. We need to veer north now, but we should be almost there. Another half an hour, maybe."

They finished eating, pulled their backpacks back on, and set off again. The trail was quiet and peaceful. Only their footsteps and the occasional crack of a twig or birdcall broke the stillness.

The deeper they went, the quieter it got.

At the two-thirty mark, Cherry stopped and held up a hand. "Smell that?"

Maisie sniffed the air. That was wood smoke. The cabin must be near. Stopping, she took off her backpack and pulled out a bottle of whisky that she'd brought with her.

Cherry raised a brow.

"Thought he might like—"

Click.

A loud, mechanical sound cut through the trees like a whipcrack.

They froze.

Slowly, Maisie turned around, heart hammering in her chest.

"Oh, Lord," whispered Cherry, clutching Maisie's arm.

In front of them, emerging from the shadowy green of the forest, stood a man with a long, weathered face and pale eyes. He was pointing a shotgun straight at them.

Chapter 15

The Mountain Man's Secret

"What do you want?" he growled.

The man Maisie took to be Jed Sutter stood a few paces ahead, the barrel of his shotgun angled low but held steady in his hands.

His face was deeply lined and weathered, his skin rough from years outdoors. A wiry grey beard framed his jaw, uneven and untrimmed, and his white hair stuck out from beneath a faded wool cap. His pale blue eyes fixed on them, sharp despite their washed-out color, watching their every movement.

"Jed Sutter?" Maisie asked, feeling Cherry's grip on her arm.

His eyes narrowed. "Who's askin'?"

"I'm Maisie and this is Cherry. We're from Thistle Grove," she added, as if that might help.

He didn't move.

"Irma told us how to find you. We just want to talk."

"What about?" he demanded, not dropping the gun.

Her pulse raced in her ears and she could feel Cherry trembling beside her. "Please, can you lower your weapon? We aren't here to hurt you."

"I'm a mom," Cherry squeaked out. For all her bravado in the woods, she was shaking like a leaf now. Then again, she had a lot to lose. "I've got an eleven-year-old daughter waiting for me, so I'd really appreciate it if you put that gun down."

Jed's gaze shifted to Cherry. He gave a nod, then slowly, lowered the weapon.

Both Maisie and Cherry let out a relieved breath.

"Thank you," Maisie said, once she'd steadied herself. The immediate threat was over, at least.

"What do you want?"

Jed's demeanor hadn't changed.

"We're sorry to bother you," she began, her voice higher pitched than usual. The scare had left her shaken. "But we wanted to ask you some questions about the Hollowells, and their baby, who went missing."

"That was a long time ago," he growled. "Sheriff already asked me about that."

"I know," Maisie said. "But we were hoping you'd talk to us about it. We want to know what you saw that day, at the mansion."

"How'd you know I was there?"

"There was a photograph," Maisie explained. "You were in it."

He gave a stiff nod.

"I didn't have nothing to do with that missing baby," he said, shuffling his feet. "I didn't take it."

"We're not saying you did," Cherry said hastily. "But you might have seen something."

Jed didn't answer right away. Instead, he looked down at the bottle of whiskey Maisie was still clutching in her hand .

"That for me?"

Maisie lifted it. "It was my grandfather's favorite brand. I thought... maybe it would be a good conversation starter."

Jed gave a grunt that might've been a laugh.

"Follow me," he said. "I've got glasses at the cabin."

Without waiting, he turned and started down the trail, his gait stiff with a faint limp. The gun dangled casually from one hand, no longer aimed but still very present.

Maisie and Cherry exchanged a look.

"He's not going to shoot us," Cherry whispered. "If he was, he'd have done so already."

"And he knows Irma knows we're here," Maisie murmured.

Cherry gave a tight nod. "Exactly."

"You coming?" Jed called over his shoulder, not bothering to stop.

They followed.

The trail wound on for several more minutes, the forest growing quieter with each step. Then, at last, the trees began to thin, and Jed's cabin came into view.

It stood in a shallow clearing, the ground covered in damp leaves and clusters of ferns. Near the center, a wide tree stump served as a chopping block, with a hatchet left half buried in a split log beside it. The cabin itself looked as though it had once been well kept, but time had worn it down. It leaned slightly to one side, its wooden walls faded to grey and streaked with moss. The roof sagged under a thick layer of fallen needles, and a crooked chimney rose into the clear blue sky.

To one side, a gnarled old apple tree stood bare and skeletal, its limbs grey and twisted like something out of one of the books Eloise was always reading.

They followed him inside.

Maisie stood at the entrance and looked around the simple cabin. There were only two rooms: a main living space that served multiple purposes, and a bedroom through an open doorway to the right.

It was minimally furnished. A sagging couch sat against one wall, its cushions worn from years of use, while a small wood stove gave off a steady, reliable heat.

Nearby, a battered kitchen basin and a pair of free-standing cupboards stood side by side, their surfaces marked by time. A handcrafted wooden bookcase stood in the corner, the shelves filled with dog-eared paperbacks.

A threadbare rug lay across the floor, dulled over time, and the whole place smelled of wood smoke, old pine and dust.

There was something sad and lonely about the cabin, even with the heat coming from the wood burner. Maisie felt a pang of sympathy. Then again, Jed had chosen this life.

"Sit," he said, motioning to a couple of chairs positioned around a worn, wooden table.

"Thank you."

They both took a seat and Maisie set the whiskey down on the table, but Jed didn't move to open it.

Cherry pulled her water bottle out and took a long gulp.

Maisie kept her gaze on Jed who overturned a wooden box and settled across from them. The shotgun was now propped beside the stove, but it was still within easy reach.

"Living free is a dying art," he muttered. Maisie glanced at Cherry but didn't say anything. "Most folks spend their whole lives trying to buy things they don't need. Big houses, new cars, gadgets. What for? You can't take it with you, can you?"

"No, sir," Cherry said.

"It must be peaceful out here," Maisie offered.

He grunted. Maisie took that to be a yes.

"Did you see anyone on the Hollowell property the day of the party?" Maisie asked.

"Plenty folk were there," he muttered.

"I mean anyone out of the ordinary," she amended.

"No."

There was a brief silence. Maisie was just thinking this was a complete waste of time, when he said softly. "I know where a baby is buried, though."

Cherry gasped, while Maisie stared at him.

"You know where the child is buried?" she asked, just to be sure she'd heard him correctly.

A nod.

"H—How?" Cherry stuttered. "Where?"

"In the woods."

"Why didn't you say anything?" Maisie asked.

"They already thought I'd done it once," he reasoned. "Didn't want them to think it again."

That made sense.

"How long ago was this?" Cherry asked, frowning.

He shrugged. "Thirty years back, give or take."

Maisie just stared at him. Jed had known where baby

Tobias was buried all this time and hadn't said a word to anyone. Not even his cousin.

"I'd never hurt anyone, least of all a child," he said.

Maisie nodded. She believed him, but the fact that he'd held on to this information didn't look very good.

"You have to tell the sheriff," she whispered.

Jed fixed his gaze on her. "They'll send me to jail."

"What if it's an anonymous tip-off?" Cherry asked, glancing at Maisie.

"He doesn't have a telephone," she pointed out, even though it was obvious.

"Not him. Us." Cherry wiggled her eyebrows. "We could pass on the information to Markham on Jed's behalf."

"We'd have to tell him where we got it," Maisie argued. "Otherwise we're obstructing an investigation."

Cherry sighed. "Okay. We're going to have to think about that." She turned back to Jed. "How did you find the body?"

"I was out walking, when I saw the ground had been disturbed. Dug up, probably by wild animals. That's when I found it."

"You saw the remains?" Maisie whispered.

"Bones," he qualified. "I saw bones."

Maisie swallowed.

Jed looked away, scuffed his boot against the wooden floor, and cleared his throat. "Should have said something, but no one would've believed me. Not after how they talked about me. I heard what they were saying."

Maisie feared he was probably right.

"Thank you for telling us," she said. This was huge. "Can you show us where he is?"

Jed sniffed. "I can give you the coordinates."

Maisie scrambled for her phone.

"You marked the spot?" Cherry asked.

He shrugged. "Didn't feel right leaving it out there completely forgotten."

As Maisie took down the coordinates, she wondered how even a loner like Jed could have held on to this knowledge for so long. Thirty years. That was a hell of a secret to live with.

Finally, for the first time since Margot's murder, she felt the stirrings of hope. Maybe the answers were slowly beginning to surface.

Three hours later, Cherry's SUV turned into the gravel parking lot of the Thistle Grove Sheriff's Department. They'd made the decision to go straight there and report what they'd found out. It was too important not to.

They were going to try not to give Markham Jed's name, though, if they could possibly help it. The old man had been through enough the first time round.

As soon as the car rolled to a stop, Maisie jumped out, then grasped the door.

"What's wrong?" Cherry asked, worried.

"I've stiffened up," she complained, letting go and tentatively taking a step towards the building.

"You really need to work out more," Cherry said, passing her on the path. "You should try roller derby. You'd get a cool nickname."

Maisie shook her head. "If this is how I feel after a hike, I dread to think how I'll feel once I've rolled around the circuit a couple of times."

Cherry laughed. "Come on. Let's go tell Markham what we know."

"Ladies," Markham said, as they walked, or in Maisie's case, hobbled, inside. "How can I help you today?"

He glanced at Maisie. "You had an accident?"

Cherry snorted. "She's just unfit. No, we're here because we have a major lead to report."

Markham eyed them curiously. "What's this about?"

"The Hollowell case," Cherry supplied.

He frowned, then gestured for them to follow him. "Come to my office. We can speak privately there."

Once seated opposite his large, document-covered desk, he steepled his fingers and said, "Explain."

Maisie took a deep breath. "We think we know where Tobias Hollowell's remains are buried."

Markham stared at her for a long moment, then his gaze flickered to Cherry, who nodded. "She's telling the truth. We spoke to someone who found them in the woods."

Markham's brows met in the middle. "Who?"

Maisie didn't miss the suspicion in his tone. This was what Jed had been afraid of.

"We can't tell you," she said.

His complexion reddened. "What do you mean? I'm the sheriff. You have to tell me."

Maisie stood her ground. "I'm sorry, Sheriff. I'd be betraying a trust if I told you. The person didn't want to be named."

He clenched his fists. "How do you know he's telling the truth."

"We believe him," Cherry said, firmly.

Markham sucked in a breath. "I'm going to need a little more proof than just your word. No offense."

Cherry tensed. This was what Maisie had been afraid of.

"We have the coordinates," she said, helpfully. "Maybe you can send one of your deputies out to check?"

Cherry slid a piece of paper with the coordinates on across to him.

Markham glanced down at it but didn't touch it. "This is a forty-year-old cold case. Why would I reopen it now based on these coordinates?"

"Don't you want to know if the infant is buried there?" Cherry asked, disbelief in her voice.

He crossed his arms and studied them. "Did it ever occur to you that whoever gave you these coordinates might be the killer?"

"We don't believe he is," Maisie reasoned.

Markham scoffed. "No offense, Ms. Button, but isn't that for a court to decide."

Maisie closed her mouth. He was right. She didn't like it, but he was right.

"Now, while I appreciate your enthusiasm, I have work to do."

"You're not even going to check it out?" Cherry demanded. Maisie flashed her a warning glance and shook her head.

"On what evidence?" He got to his feet. "You can't even tell me who supplied you with this information. Without that, I have no proof. Just your word."

"But... but..." Cherry stuttered. "There could be a baby buried out there."

"If your source really believes this is legitimate, he should come into the station. I will decide if it's worth following up on, otherwise, I have more pressing matters to attend to."

"Come on," Maisie said to Cherry, gesturing for them to leave. "Let's go."

It was outside that they bumped into MJ.

"What's wrong?" she said, taking one look at their faces. "Has something happened?"

"We found something, but the sheriff won't take us seriously," Cherry fumed.

"Found what?" She gasped. "Did Jed Sutter know something?"

Maisie nodded and told her about the remains and the coordinates. "He won't act on it until we give him our source. Jed asked us specifically not to mention his name. He was worried he'd be the most obvious suspect."

MJ frowned. "Was Andy there?"

"Who?" Cherry asked.

"Deputy Summers," MJ corrected.

"I think so," Maisie nodded. "I spotted him briefly as we walked in."

MJ put a hand on Cherry's sleeve. "Leave this with me."

And she strode off in the direction of the sheriff's department.

Maisie was soaking her exhausted muscles in the tub when her phone rang. Glancing down, she saw it was MJ.

"Hey, how'd it go with Deputy Summers?" she asked, once she'd answered.

"He's agreed to look into the coordinates," MJ told her.

"Really? That's great. How did you get him to come around?" Maisie asked.

"I pointed out how good it would be for his career if he solved a forty-year-old case."

Maisie laughed. "That's genius. I wish I'd thought of that."

"Markham still isn't on board, but Andy is going to speak to someone at Rutherford Timber. One of their guys is going to take a look. If they find something, they'll let him know."

"Excellent," Maisie breathed. "At least we can help solve that mystery, if not who killed Margot."

"One step at a time," MJ said. "One step at a time."

Chapter 16

What's A Filbert?

"Where's MJ?" Eloise asked from the rocker, as she stroked Mewsly's furry belly.

It was Monday evening, and the Knit and Natter group had assembled at Tangled Threads for their after work catch-up.

Everybody, except MJ, was sitting around the farmhouse table, and Maisie could feel the anticipation in the air.

"She's got a date tonight," Cherry told her daughter.

"A date? With who?" Eloise asked.

"Whom," Ree corrected automatically.

"Whom," Eloise mimicked with a grin.

"Jesse Turner," Maisie confided. "I think they make a cute couple."

"He's soft on her for sure." Ree nodded.

"Jesse from the garden center?" Bev asked, eyebrows shooting up. "He's such a sweetheart. Does the flowers for the town hall."

"We don't have any baked good this evening," Eloise noted, eyeing the table.

What with the hike and then an early morning start, Maisie hadn't had time to bake, and the store had been too busy today to dash out and buy any.

She got to her feet. "Luckily Dillard's is right next door. I'll go grab some now."

"Please, don't worry on El's account," Cherry said, shooting a stern look at her daughter.

"Oh, please do worry," Ree countered, grinning.

"I could handle a snack," Brian admitted, patting his stomach.

Maisie laughed. "You're outnumbered Cherry. I'll be right back. Don't start without me." She set her knitting on the table and headed for the door.

Dillard's was still open, so Maisie pushed open the door and went inside. The tiny bell above the door gave a friendly tinkle.

"Evening, Maisie," Harvey called, wiping his hands on his apron.

"Hi Harvey," she replied, side-stepping June Penrose as she hurried out. "Oh. Excuse me, June."

June gave her a polite nod but kept walking.

"What can I get you?" he asked, sounding tired.

"You okay?" He was usually so jovial and upbeat.

"Yeah. Monday's are always busy—and I was up at three."

"I struggle to get up at seven," she told him, pulling a face.

"Fifteen years. You'd think it'd get easier." He grimaced. "Do you know I go to bed at eight o'clock every night?"

"But you make the best cinnamon buns in three counties," Maisie said, trying to cheer him up. "So it's totally worth it. Speaking of which..."

"Let me guess," Harvey reached for a pastry box. "Something sweet for the knitting circle?"

"Please, and a marionberry pie, if that's what I'm seeing there." Maisie nodded toward the display case. "It's my new obsession."

"You and everyone else's," Harvey said as he began assembling the boxes. Maisie read the Easter menu on the painted chalkboard while she waited, and inhaled the fresh aroma of bread, sugar and cinnamon. It smelled like heaven.

Her stomach let out a loud rumble, but thankfully Harvey didn't seem to notice. She was glad she'd been persuaded to come over and pick up some treats.

"Here you go." Harvey stacked two pastry boxes on the counter. "That'll be twenty-two."

Maisie handed over her card and waited while he processed her payment.

"Thanks, Harvey. See you tomorrow."

His eyes creased at the corners. "I'll be here."

"Harvey was in a weird mood this evening," Maisie told the others, as she unpacked the baked goods.

"Ooh, I *love* filberts," Ree said, fishing a brownie from the pastry box.

Bev raised her eyebrows. "I haven't heard that name in a while."

Eloise blinked. "What's a filbert?"

"It's a hazelnut," Ree explained, before taking a bite and closing her eyes in ecstasy. "So good."

"So why do you call them a filbert?" Eloise asked, frowning.

"It's a local thing," Ree said with her mouth full. "I don't really know why."

"Grandma used to call them that too," Cherry remembered with a fond smile. "She made chocolate-filbert tarts every Christmas."

Maisie frowned at the pastries. "That's so strange. I asked Harvey for cinnamon buns and marionberry pie. Not hazelnut brownies."

"No complaints from me," said Ree, taking another bite. The sentiment was echoed around the table with approving hums and nods.

Maisie gave a small shrug. Harvey must have been more distracted than she'd thought.

"Okay, let's get down to business," she said, taking a sweat. "We've got a lot to discuss."

"Starting with Jed Sutter," Bev said. "I heard you found him."

"Oh, we did," Cherry nodding, brushing crumbs from her mouth. "But that's not all we found."

"Did he tell you anything?" Brian asked.

"Better than that," Cherry met her gaze. Maisie nodded, as if to say, go ahead. Cherry leaned forward. "He found a body. Baby Tobias's body."

There was a collective gasp.

"Where?" Brian blurted out.

"H—How?" Ree stammered.

"What?" Bev snapped.

"In the Rutherford forest," Maisie explained once the initial uproar had died down. "Jed said he came across the grave thirty years ago while he was out walking. It had been dug up by wild animals, that's how he noticed it."

"Why didn't he report it then?" Ree asked, incredulous.

"He was scared," Cherry said. "The sheriff already thought he was guilty because he was there that day. He thought they'd lock him up and throw away the key."

"Do you think he's telling the truth?" Bev asked, her investigator's brain considering all the options.

"I believed him," Maisie said, glancing at Cherry.

She nodded in agreement. "We spent time with him. He's a little rough around the edges, but I don't think he was lying. Besides, if he was involved with the kidnapping, why would he point us toward the grave?"

"That's what I was thinking," Brian said. "He didn't have to say anything, yet he still decided to tell you about it."

"He even gave us coordinates," Cherry told them. "First thing we did when we got back was to hand them to the sheriff."

Bev's eyebrows lifted. "Sheriff Markham is going to send someone out to find the remains?"

"He wasn't going to at first," Maisie admitted, breaking into a smile. "But thanks to MJ's powers of persuasion, Deputy Andy is going to pass the coordinates to Rutherford Timber who are going to check it out."

"That deputy is sweet on MJ too," Ree said with a knowing nod. "Felicity from the book club told me."

Brian clapped his hands. "Well done, MJ."

"This could be the breakthrough we've been waiting for," Bev said slowly. "If those are baby Tobias's remains, at least we'll know how he died."

"I'm not sure I want to know," Ree said, shaking her head.

Maisie knew how she felt.

"We still don't know who took him," she pointed out. "Or who killed Margot."

"But we are assuming the two murders are connected?" Brian asked, looking around the group.

"They must be," Cherry said. "If Margot discovered who the killer was, they'd want to silence her."

"The answer must be in the tapestry," Eloise said, turning around to take another look at it.

Brian frowned at it. "We're missing something."

"I agree with El," Cherry said, nodding at the weaving loom. "We already figured out that the figure in the flames was Ada Hollowell holding Tobias. The initials TH and the sycamore tree back that up."

"So what aren't we seeing?" Bev asked, twisting in her seat.

Maisie stared at the rich townscape, her gaze drifting to the church. "I keep circling back to that upside-down cross. At first I thought it was about Margot looking up Tobias's birth record at the church, but maybe it's got to do with the land deal and the differing deeds."

"Did you speak to Harriet about it?" Ree asked.

Maisie nodded. "She was as confused as we were. She couldn't account for it at all."

"Then it's back to Father Tom. I'll pay him another visit tomorrow." Brain patted his head. "Oh, shoot. I forgot we've got a training day at the library."

"Don't worry," Maisie said. "Tuesdays are pretty quiet in the store. I'll go."

The Hazelnut Brownie Complication

Maisie woke with a groan.

"That'll teach me for not keeping up with my cardio," she grumbled to Mewsly, who opened her slit-eyes, gave her a 'this is your own fault' look, and went back to sleep.

"Thanks for the sympathy," she muttered, lowering herself gingerly to the floor. Maybe some stretching would help.

She sat on the floor, legs out in front of her, and bent over to touch her toes. It wasn't easy.

Neither was getting up.

With limbs a little less stiff, she hobbled into the kitchen in search of coffee. The sky beyond the kitchen window was an enthusiastic blue, raising her spirits.

Flipping on the coffee maker, she reached for her

phone. There was one person she wanted to check in with before she did anything else. MJ.

Maisie knew she'd be at work already. The diner opened early. If she was lucky, she'd catch her on a break.

How did the date go?

As soon as she set her phone down, a small, demanding meow rose up behind her.

Mewsly, the queen of breakfast dramatics, was waiting by her bowl. Anyone would think she was starving.

Maisie scooped out a portion of wet food and crouched down to drop it into her bowl, then wished she hadn't. Mewsly purred and tucked in.

Maisie let out a low hiss and gripped the cupboard handle, as she contemplated whether her thighs would allow her to get up again.

"What? It was that uphill bit, okay," she said in response to Mewsly's perturbed look.

Hauling herself to her feet, she ate her own breakfast and washed it down with a cup of coffee.

"What mischief are you planning today?" she asked her cat, as Mewsly weaved in and out of her legs. "More neighborly visits? You've been invited into more homes than I have."

Mewsly looked up, her expression unreadable.

Maisie narrowed her eyes as a thought occurred to her. "Is that why you're getting so fat? Are you charming snacks out of everyone in Thistle Grove?"

Before Mewsly could confirm or deny the charges, Maisie's phone buzzed. She glanced down at the text message. It was from MJ.

He stood me up 🙁

"What?" Maisie said aloud. That couldn't be right.

Last night, on her way home from the store, she'd seen

Jesse's charcoal pickup drive by. She was sure of it. Frowning, she tapped out another message.

What happened?

MJ's reply was swift.

He didn't even call. Still hasn't.

Maisie tsked, causing Mewsly to look up expectantly.

"No, I'm not calling you," Maisie murmured, as she typed:

I'm so sorry. You deserve better!

She stared at the phone for a moment longer, as if willing more answers to appear, but it seemed MJ was done typing.

Maisie leaned back in her chair and drummed her fingers on the kitchen table. Jesse was many things—friendly, genuine, hardworking—but *flaky* he was not. He was one of the most dependable people she knew.

"That's really strange," she murmured to Mewsly, then winced as she stood up. "Something must have happened."

By the time she was ready to leave the house, the temperature had risen and the sun was shining. It was shaping up to be a warm spring day.

"Are you coming?" she asked Mewsly as she opened the door.

Mewsly blinked her green-gold eyes and flicked her tail but didn't move.

"Okay, then. Fine." Maisie made to close the door. "I can't wait for you to make your mind up. I have a store to open. Customers to serve."

Mewsly shot forward, just making it out before the door closed.

Maisie gave a soft snort. "Works every time."

She was still smiling as she drove into town, but it faded when she pulled up in front of Tangled Threads.

What was Sheriff Markham's cruiser doing here?

The sheriff and Deputy Andy were standing outside Dillard's Bakehouse, somber expressions on their faces.

Maisie's heart gave an odd little skip as she noticed the bakery's sign wasn't on and the windows were shrouded in darkness. Harvey had said he was going to be here today.

"Ms. Button," Sheriff Markham called as she climbed out of the car. "Can we have a word?"

Maisie hurried over. "Where's Harvey? Is everything okay?"

"No, ma'am. I'm afraid it's not." He nodded toward the darkened bakery. "Harvey Dillard was killed last night."

Maisie felt the world tilt. She reached out and grabbed his arm for support. "What?"

"Suspected hit-and-run," he said, his gaze dropping to her hand. "Happened late last night."

Her mouth fell open. "No, that can't be right. I saw him yesterday afternoon. We talked. He packed up pastries for me."

"What time was that?" Markham asked.

Deputy Andy came out of the bakery and stood beside them. "No sigh of anyone going inside, sheriff."

Markham nodded. "Okay, lock it up."

Maisie tried to think but her mind was racing. Harvey dead? A hit and run? She couldn't believe this was really happening?

"Miss Button?" Markham prodded.

"Sorry." She ran a hand through her head and tried to think. "It was early evening, around six o'clock. I was buying some pastries for our knitting circle."

"Did you notice anything unusual?" Markham asked. "About Mr. Dillard, I mean."

Maisie hesitated as she remembered the filberts. "Actually, yes. He seemed a little...off."

Markham frowned. "What do you mean, off?"

"You know? Not himself. Distracted. He gave me the wrong order, and he didn't even notice."

"Wrong order how?" asked the deputy, scribbling.

"I asked for cinnamon buns and marionberry pie. He gave me filberts—hazelnut brownies—instead. Even though the buns were right there in the display case."

Markham blinked at her, then turned his attention to her car. "Do you mind if I take a look at your vehicle?"

"My car? Why?" Then it clicked. "Are you serious? You think I hit Harvey?"

"It's standard procedure," he replied. "You were one of the last few people to see him alive."

She gulped as the thought sent a chill down her spine.

"If I'd hit him, I'd have stopped," she retorted, then decided she didn't want to even consider that situation.

Markham ignored her and strode over to her car to inspect it.

"You're wasting your time, Sheriff," she called after him. Okay, she was getting annoyed now. What did he think she was? "I didn't hit Harvey. I think I would've *noticed* if I had. Besides, I was home all evening. What time did you say he was killed?"

"I didn't," he barked back.

Maisie's temper flared, but she swallowed it. "Well, I didn't see anything when I left the store."

She watched as Markham began inspecting her vehicle. Deputy Andy finished locking up the bakery, then returned.

"Get the names of everyone in that knitting circle," Markham said to him. "The ones who were here last night."

"Sorry, Maisie," Andy said, turning to her. He'd taken a notepad and pen out of his back pocket. "I need everybody's name."

She gave a weary nod. "You going to inspect their vehicles too?"

"We have to. We're just doing our jobs," he explained.

"I know. I'm sorry. It's just that Harvey was a friend."

"Oh, I didn't know. I'm sorry for your loss," Andy said, putting a hand on her shoulder. "Are you okay?"

"Brian, Ree—or rather, Iris—, Bev, Cherry and her daughter Eloise. MJ wasn't there last night."

"Where was she?" he asked, still glancing at his pad.

"She was supposed to be on a date," Maisie replied, then bit her tongue as Andy stilled.

Darn it. She'd forgotten he was soft on MJ too.

"But he stood her up," she added quickly. "It never happened."

"Who with?" he asked.

Maisie hesitated. "Jesse Turner."

Andy nodded and made a note on his pad. "So, he could have been out driving too?"

Maisie shrugged. "I don't know."

Then an icicle slid down her spine. Could that be the reason why Jesse hadn't turned up for their date? He'd mistakenly hit Harvey.

She sucked in a breath. Surely not?

Not Jesse. He'd never have kept driving if that was the case. He just wasn't like that.

"I'll have to talk to them all," Andy said. "Even Jesse."

Maisie nodded. These were her friends. None of them were responsible. She felt as certain of that as she did of her own innocence.

None of this made any sense.

"What was Harvey even doing out at that time?" she asked, suddenly.

Andy frowned. "What do you mean?"

"Well, he's always home in bed by eight. He told me himself. He gets up at three to start baking."

Andy stared at her. "You sure about that?"

"Positive. He told me that he's exhausted in the evenings."

Markham returned and gave Andy a nod. "No visible damage on the Honda."

"Well, what do you know?" Maisie couldn't resist saying.

Chapter 18

Jesse's Confession

Maisie opened up the store, but she was moving on autopilot. She flipped the lights on, started the coffee maker, but instead of making one for herself, she brewed a cup of chamomile tea.

When it was ready, she sat down at the farmhouse table and wrapped her hands around the mug. Outside the sun beat down, as if mocking her. Not such a beautiful day, after all, she thought, glaring outside at the flashing lights of the sheriff's vehicles.

Taking a few slow breaths, she tried to center herself.

The steam from her tea curled around her like a soft herbal blanket. Through the glass, she could hear the deep timbre of Sheriff Markham's voice as he issued commands. Trying to tune him out, she attempted to make sense of what had happened, but there didn't seem to be any sense to be made.

Oh, Harvey. She gave a ragged gasp and blinked back tears.

This wasn't just grief. She knew that feeling well by now—the jagged, sorrowful tide that came in waves after losing Frankie. No, this was something colder. Sharper. The way her gut twisted didn't feel like mourning. It felt like dread.

Because Harvey Dillard hadn't been the kind of man to walk the streets late at night. Not when he was exhausted from a long day and a three o'clock start.

So why had he been out?

Had he been meeting someone? Had he forgotten to turn off an oven at the bakery? Where had he been hit? Sheriff Markham hadn't said and she'd been too stunned to ask.

Her vacant gaze shifted to Vivienne, the display mannequin, who stared blankly back. It occurred to her that Vivienne was still dressed for winter.

"You need a makeover," she said, pushing herself up off the chair. Her legs still ached, but she almost welcomed the pain. It stopped her thinking about Harvey, just for a second.

Maisie walked over and adjusted the scarf around Vivienne's stiff, pale neck. It gave her an excuse to peek outside without looking suspicious.

Deputy Andy was on the sidewalk, clipboard in hand, stopping the occasional passer-by. Sheriff Markham stood near the cruiser, phone pressed to his ear, his brow drawn in concentration. Maisie re-fluffed Vivienne's shawl, then stepped back.

Why were they still here? Was this where Harvey had been run over?

In the Main Street, outside his own bakery?

A chill swept through her and she wrapped her arms around herself. That's why Andy wanted to interview all of them. Because they'd been in the vicinity last night.

A few minutes later, the sheriff's cruiser pulled away taking their witness statements with them. The sidewalk cleared and the street went still again. Nothing much happened on Tuesdays.

Maisie thought about her trip to the bakery yesterday. Harvey definitely hadn't been himself. Was it just exhaustion like he'd said, or was there something else going on? Had something been worrying him?

The front door swept open, making her jump. She turned to see MJ stride in, concern etched across her face.

"I just heard. Isn't it terrible? Poor Harvey."

Maisie let out a ragged sob, her hand going to her mouth.

MJ embraced her and they stood together for a moment, drawing mutual comfort.

Eventually, Maisie extracted herself. "I'm okay. It was just a shock, that's all."

MJ nodded. "Totally understandable. Harvey was... well, he was part of our community. We'll all miss him."

Maisie gulped down a sob, determined not to cry again. "I don't understand why he was out walking last night when he told me he was going home."

"He said that?" MJ asked, frowning.

"Well, not in so many words. He said he'd had a long, busy day and was tired. That he woke up at three every morning to start baking." She shook her head. "Why would he go out again?"

"Andy asked me where I was last night," MJ confided. "That must be when Harvey got hit."

Maisie nodded.

"Who would do that?" MJ asked. "I mean, who hits someone and doesn't stop? Doesn't check?" Her voice cracked with disbelief.

Maisie just shrugged. She didn't know what to say.

MJ slumped down at the farmhouse table. "You're right, though. It is strange that he was out so late."

Maisie joined her. "What's even stranger is that he mixed up my order yesterday."

"What order?" MJ asked.

"Of course. You weren't here. I stopped by to pick up some pastries for last night's meeting. He gave me the wrong thing. Totally mixed it up."

"That's not like him," MJ agreed, then she scowled. "I should have come, but I was waiting for that dumbass, Jesse."

That drew Maisie's thoughts from Harvey.

Blinking to clear her eyes, she asked, "Did you find out why he stood you up?"

MJ shook her head. "Not a word. Can you believe it?"

Maisie bit her lip. "Honestly, I can't. I never thought he was like that."

MJ exhaled noisily. "Just goes to show, you can never tell with some people."

She wasn't wrong there.

Mewsly weaved between them under the table, meowing. She probably sensed something was up.

MJ's phone rang.

"What the hell?" she muttered, staring at it.

"Who is it?" Maisie asked.

"Jesse."

"Take it."

Maisie moved away to give her some privacy.

"Now you call me," MJ snapped, her voice like steel. "Well, I'm not interested in excuses."

Maisie cringed, and tried not to listen, but it was impossible. MJ was talking loudly, her voice carrying across the store.

"You're where?"

Maisie glanced up to see her friend pale. Frowning, she started back towards her.

"What are you doing at the sheriff's department?"

Maisie's heart sank.

"What? You're in jail? Why?"

The hit-and-run. It had to be.

She saw MJ's eyes widen and knew she was right.

MJ stared helplessly at her, then hit the 'speaker' button. Jesse's shaky voice filled the store.

"They're saying I killed Harvey. I don't know what to do. I've tried calling my aunt, but she isn't picking up."

"Why would they think that?" MJ demanded, her hand clenched around the phone.

"I don't know but they've impounded my truck." Jesse swallowed a sob. "They're claiming I hit him and kept driving. I thought I'd hit a pothole. I swear, I didn't see Harvey. I never would've kept going if I'd known."

"Jesse, it's Maisie," Maisie said, stepping in. "Take a deep breath and try to keep calm. Can you tell us exactly what happened."

They heard Jesse exhale. When he spoke, his voice sounded sightly calmer. "I was driving home last night when I went over a bump in the road. It didn't seem big enough to worry about. Sure didn't feel like a human. I would have known."

"Driving home from where?" MJ asked.

He didn't reply.

"Where were you last night, Jesse?" she repeated. "You never showed up for our date."

The silence stretched out. Then, Jesse said, "There was something I had to do. I'm sorry. I should've called, but... I was upset. I let it get to me."

"Let what get to you?" MJ's tone was sharp now, more hurt than angry.

"I can't talk about it. Not right now," Jesse said. "Can we discuss it later?"

"Of course you can," Maisie said, cutting off MJ who was about to retort. "Right now you need a lawyer. Do you know anyone, Jesse?"

"No." His voice was tinged with hysteria. "They said I can get a public defender, but I haven't met him yet."

"I'll find someone and send them over," Maisie said, hoping to reassure him. "In the meantime, don't talk to anyone."

"What about the sheriff?" he asked.

"No one," Maisie reiterated firmly.

"Maisie, am I going to prison?" His voice cracked.

MJ shot an alarmed look at Maisie.

"Not if we can help it," she said. "I'll meet the lawyer at the sheriff's department. Try not to worry. We'll figure this out."

"Thanks, Maisie." He sounded close to tears.

"Don't mention it."

She ended the call but MJ just sat staring at her phone. "I can't believe this. Jesse, of all people."

"I know. It's crazy." Maisie strode toward the cash register. "I know someone I can call, then we'll head over to the department."

"This is bad, isn't it?" MJ whispered.

Maisie didn't meet her gaze. "Let's see what the lawyer says, before we assume the worst."

Maisie closed the store and they met the lawyer, a no-nonsense woman named Alana Perez, at the sheriff's department two hours later. A friend had given her the woman's details after Frank had died, to sort out all the legal stuff she'd had to deal with.

"I've spoken with the sheriff and Jesse," Perez told them when they arrived. "I won't sugar-coat it. Jesse is looking at a possible manslaughter charge. At least he wasn't driving under the influence or it might be a lot worse."

"What's worse than manslaughter?" MJ whispered, clutching Maisie's arm.

"Vehicular homicide, for one," Perez replied.

Maisie patted MJ's hand. "It's not going to come to that. He didn't even know he'd hit anyone."

"It's whether a jury will believe that," Perez reasoned.

"They have to believe it," MJ blurted out. "It's the truth."

"Let's see what the medical examiner has to say," Perez said.

Maisie knew that would be the deciding factor.

"I have to call Jesse's aunt," MJ said. "I've already left four messages." She'd just walked off to make the call, when Sheriff Markham came out of his office.

He gestured to Perez.

"Excuse me. I'll be right back." She walked over to him.

Maisie stood by the door, a heaviness in her chest that she couldn't shift. First Margot, now Henry. Two seemingly unrelated events. How was that even possible?

The sheriff was talking in a low voice, his head bowed, while Perez nodded repeatedly. When he finished, she marched back over, a grin on her face.

"What was that about?" she asked.

"Jesse's free to go," Perez said.

Maisie blinked. "You mean he's out on bail?"

"Nope. I mean he's free. Period. Sheriff Markham just got the medical examiner's report and it confirms Jesse's vehicle did make contact with Harvey Dillard."

Maisie shook her head. "I don't understand. If he made contact, how is he exonerated?" Surely that was confirmation of the hit-and-run accident.

Perez wore a smug look. "The cause of death was blunt force trauma to the head."

"That could have been from Jesse's pickup," Maisie began.

"The back of his head," Perez corrected. "And in the shape of a hammer."

Maisie stared at her. "Oh."

Perez rested her hand on Maisie's shoulder. "It wasn't him. There was no blood on the Jesse's truck. Harvey was dead before Jesse hit him with his pickup."

"Oh, thank goodness," she breathed, then gasped. "I don't mean thank goodness Harvey's dead, just—"

"I know. Don't worry about it." Perez gave the professional smile of someone who'd seen it all before.

Maisie rubbed her temples. "Wait. Does that mean someone hit Harvey on the head with a hammer, then dragged his body into the street and left him there?"

Perez nodded. "Yeah. To make it look like an accident."

Maisie exhaled. "That's awful. Who would do something like that?"

"That," Perez said, "is a job for the sheriff's department. I'm going to go now. You should be okay from here on out."

"Thank you," Maisie said, shaking her hand.

"No problem. I didn't do anything." She grinned. "I'm glad it worked out."

Sheriff Markham walked over to them. "Thought you might like to know my deputy is getting Mr. Turner ready for release. We still need a statement from him, but he's no longer a suspect in Harvey Dillard's death."

Maisie let out a relieved sigh, and went to tell MJ, who was still on the phone to Jesse's aunt.

She shrieked and relayed the information into the phone.

Margot flashed her a smile and walked away. While she was relieved at the outcome for Jesse, she still felt a horrible sense of dread. Someone in Thistle Grove had killed Margot and now Harvey. And they were still out there.

Chapter 19

A Stark Realization

"I can't thank you enough for your help," Jesse said, as they left the sheriff's department and walked to Maisie's car.

"I'm just glad they cleared you," Maisie said. "What an ordeal."

"I've never been in jail before." he looked pale, hollowed out by the stress of the past few hours. "I hope never to repeat the experience." His gaze flicked to MJ who stood stiffly a few feet away. She looked past him, not at him.

"I've got to go," she said, "I'm due at the diner." And strode off down the street.

Jesse started to go after her, but Maisie laid a hand on his arm. "Give her some time," she advised. "She's also had a shock."

He watched her go and then nodded. "I really messed that up, didn't I"?"

"Where were you last night?" Maisie asked, as she unlocked her Honda. "I'm sorry, I don't mean to pry, but I think it's important you tell her."

He opened the door with a sigh. "It's personal, okay. I didn't mean to stand MJ up, but something important came up and... my plans suddenly changed."

"You should have let her know," Maisie chided, getting in.

"I know." He climbed into the passenger seat, his head hung low. "I feel bad about it, but I wasn't thinking straight."

They drove past MJ who was striding along the sidewalk towards the diner and turned into Main Street. A short time later, they were pulling up outside Tangled Threads.

As they got out of the car, Maisie glanced next door at Dillard's Bakehouse, still in darkness. The crooked *Closed* sign still hung in the window, just as Harvey had left it. Deputy Andy hadn't disturbed it when he'd gone in for a preliminary search.

A pang made her catch her breath. The tears started to well again, but she blinked them away. There was no point in crying. The best thing she could do was find out who'd killed Harvey, and why.

Her gaze cut across the street to the corner of Grover Avenue and Main, where Margot's white weatherboard house sat tucked behind a low hedge and an overgrown rhododendron bush. The red door, once so cheerful, now seemed to sulk in its frame.

She sighed. Another home without its heart.

Margot had always joked that living across the road from the bakehouse was both a blessing and a curse. "Too many cinnamon rolls, not enough self-control," she'd once told her.

Maisie choked back a sob and turned to go inside— when a thought struck her. She froze. Then slowly swiveled around, her eyes locked on the bakery.

Dillard's was diagonally across the street from Margot's. So close that Harvey, if he'd looked up from kneading or glazing or packaging bread, might have seen something over the road. Or someone.

She sat with the thought for a moment, her pulse ticking up a notch.

Could Harvey have seen Margot's killer?

The sheriff hadn't shared her exact time of death, but Maisie knew it had to fall between 2 a.m.—when Margot had sent that cryptic text about her journal—and the time Maisie had stopped by the next morning.

Harvey, she knew, would have been at the bakery from just after three o'clock, working in the pre-dawn hours.

Her breath caught. Was that the link they'd been missing? Had Harvey witnessed something, or someone, slinking down Grover Avenue or slipping through Margot's gate?

She shook her head. Was this crazy? Had the shock of another death sent her brain into overdrive? Maybe she was seeing things that weren't there? Trying to manufacture reasons where there were none.

A car rattled by and still she didn't move. The thought wouldn't leave her.

Maybe Harvey hadn't even realized what he'd seen.

But the killer did.

She raised a hand to her mouth, her heart hammering. Then, all these weeks later, Harvey ended up dead. His murder staged to look like a hit and run.

Maisie turned her back on the store and crossed the street, heading for the corner.

"Maisie?" Jesse called, confused. "Where are you going?"

She held up a hand. "I'll be right back."

She walked to Margot's house and stopped out front.

Bev was walking down the street, a shopping bag in her hands. "Maisie? What are you doing?"

She didn't reply.

Bev came to a halt beside her and glanced from her to Margot's house.

"You okay? You look like you've seen a ghost."

Spinning around, Maisie stared across the street at the bakehouse.

"Margot lives diagonally opposite the bakery," she whispered, her gaze on the bakehouse window.

"Yes." Bev frowned and set down her shopping bag. "So?"

"There's a direct line of sight between the two places."

Bev looked at the bakehouse, then turned back to Margot's. Her gaze narrowed as the realization dawned.

"Are you suggesting that Harvey knew who Margot's killer was?"

Maisie gripped Bev's arm. "It makes sense, doesn't it? Henry arrived at work a little after three—he told me himself. If he'd been looking across the street at that time, he may have seen the killer sneak into her house. Or leave." Her grip tightened. "Either way, he could have gotten a glimpse."

"That's why he had to die," Bev muttered, nodding in agreement. "The murderer knew there was a chance Harvey could identify them."

"Tell me I'm not making this up," Maisie whispered,

letting go of Bev's arm. Outside Tangled Threads, Jesse was still watching them, his head at an angle, a confused expression on his face.

"You're not making this up," she decided. "It's a legitimate theory."

Maisie exhaled.

"If he'd seen the killer, that would make Harvey a witness. A threat," Bev continued.

And in the twisted, panicked logic of a murderer...

That was enough of a reason to kill.

By the time the Knit and Natter group had gathered around the farmhouse table that evening, the atmosphere was electric. Nobody had even bothered with coffee, or any baked goods, and the usual hum of laughter and chatter was conspicuously absent.

Everybody had heard about Harvey's hit-and-run, Jesse's involvement, and the ME's verdict. In a small town like this one, that kind of news spread fast.

"So he was dead before Jesse hit him with his truck," Brian clarified.

Maisie nodded. "It appears that way."

"It's too terrible for words," Ree whispered.

MJ was quiet, having come straight over from her afternoon shift at the diner, and Maisie knew she wouldn't have had a chance to speak to Jesse again yet.

"Maisie's made a breakthrough," Bev said, her throaty voice resonating around the room.

All eyes turned to her.

Maisie took a deep breath. "Two murders in the course of two weeks," she said slowly. "Seemingly unconnected."

"Seemingly?" Cherry lifted a brow.

On the rocker, Eloise was hugging Mewsly like her life depended on it, and for once, the tabby didn't seem to mind.

"I mean, what are the chances?" Maisie continued, looking around the group. "This is Thistle Grove. The murder rate isn't exactly high here."

"Not normally," Eloise blurted out.

"You're saying the same person who killed Margot, also killed Harvey?" Ree whispered.

She nodded.

"But why?" Brian murmured. "Are you saying we have a serial killer on the loose?"

"Not exactly a serial killer," Maisie replied. "But I do think someone's willing to kill to keep their secrets buried."

"I don't understand." Cherry placed her hands on the table. "How are they connected?"

"That's what I figured out today," Maisie said, standing up and going to the window. All gazes followed her.

"Harvey kept early hours, we know that. He was always at the bakery a little after three in the morning. The bake-house is across the road from Margot's. If Margot was killed sometime between her text to me, which came in at two o'clock, and when I found her at eight-thirty, that puts Harvey right in the timeframe."

Cherry gasped. "He saw something!"

Maisie nodded. "Not necessarily the murder itself, but he could have seen someone going to or leaving from Margot's house."

"The killer," Eloise whispered, clutching Mewsly so hard she let out a plaintive meow.

The group fell silent, considering the possibility.

"Wouldn't Harvey have been in the kitchen at the back of the store?" Brian asked, stroking his beard.

"For the most part," Bev agreed. "But not when he arrived, or when he was setting up the store. He would have brought the baked items from the back into the front section to display them. There are a number of possibilities."

"If someone walked by at that hour, Harvey would have noticed," Cherry added. "My dad used to work the night shift. He always said that when the rest of the world is asleep, the smallest things stand out."

"That makes sense," MJ agreed, speaking for the first time.

"But Margot was killed days ago," Ree reasoned with a little shake of her head. "Why didn't Harvey say anything sooner?"

"He may not have known what he'd seen," Maisie mused.

"But the killer sure did," Cherry finished.

Bev gave a grave nod. "If Harvey connected the dots, he could have identified the murderer."

"That's why they targeted him," Cherry whispered.

"Diabolical," Brian muttered, taking off his glasses and rubbing his eyes. "Completely unhinged."

"I think Harvey realized last night," Maisie continued, coming to sit back down. "That's why he was so distracted. And that's why he swerved me the incorrect items."

"The filbert," Eloise piped up.

Maisie nodded.

"Makes sense." MJ straightened up.

"It does," Bev agreed.

The room grew still as they all processed what she'd said.

MJ broke the silence.

"We've spent so much time chasing threads in that

tapestry, and we're still no closer to finding out what Margot knew. If only we had, we might have saved Henry."

Maisie reached over and squeezed her hand. "I know, but we're closer now than we've ever been. I feel it."

"Maisie's right," Cherry added. "Don't give up now, MJ. We're nearly there."

"We just need to stay focused," Bev added. "In my experience, all it takes is one little thing for everything to fall into place. And that can happen when you least expect it. We just have to keep digging."

"I'm not sure how much more can we learn from the tapestry," Ree said, softly. "We've studied every stitch and every symbol. How many more times can we look at it and expect to see something new?"

"Maybe the answer isn't in the tapestry," Brian said.

"What do you mean?" MJ asked.

He glanced at Maisie. "Did you talk to Father Tom again?"

Maisie shook her head. "I meant to. But with everything that happened—"

"Probably wouldn't have helped anyway," Ree whispered. "I can't see him being our killer. Two people?" She shook her head. "I can't imagine him murdering one."

Maisie stared down at the table. "I feel like we've got most of the pieces to the puzzle, so why can't we see the full picture?"

"Maybe we're too close to it," Brian suggested. "Sometimes you need distance to see the whole design."

"Maybe," Maisie murmured.

"We can't give up," Cherry said, slapping her hands down on the table and waking them all up. "We won't."

"Margot wouldn't want us to," Ree said, wiping her eyes.

Bev glanced at them all in turn. "So we press on, and we figure this thing out."

They all nodded.

Maisie drew in a steadying breath. They were right. They had to keep going. For Margot. For Harvey. And for baby Tobias.

Whatever it took, they'd get to the bottom of these murders. The killer was not going to get away with what they'd done. Not if she had anything to do with it. Not in her town.

Chapter 20

The Question Remains

Maisie stood at the farmhouse table folding colorful quarts of fabric, when the door burst open and MJ rushed in. Mewsly, who'd been enjoying a nap in the sunshine, darted out of the door, but not before shooting MJ a disgruntled look.

It was a crisp spring day, with blue skies and a chill in the air. MJ looked suitably arty in a teal sweater-dress over a pair of gray leggings, and a multicolored scarf looped around her neck.

"Not working at the diner today?" Maisie asked.

"Later," she replied, heading straight for the coffee maker. "I couldn't sleep a wink. I just kept thinking about what you said, about the two murders being linked. Eventually, my mom said I should get out of the house before I start climbing the walls."

That made two of them. Maisie had tossed and turned all night too, thinking about the case. About the breakthrough they'd had, and how it still didn't make it any clearer.

"How's it going at home?" She asked. MJ was living with her parents while she decided what to do with her life.

MJ gave a small shrug. "It's okay. My mom says she doesn't mind me living there while I figure things out, but every other day she's asking when I'm going back to school or getting a proper job."

"You are working at the diner," Maisie murmured.

"That's not full time," she said with a sigh and slumped down at the opposite end of the table with her giant mug of coffee.

"What about your dad?" Maisie asked, watching as MJ took a loud slurp and closed her eyes.

"He's been pretty supportive," she replied. "He was the one who pushed me to study business, so when I dropped out, it didn't go down too well."

Maisie grimaced.

"But I think he's beginning to see that was never me."

Maisie gave a sympathetic grin. "You're smart and creative, MJ, but I just can't picture you in a cubicle, wading through quarterly reports."

MJ crinkled her nose. "Neither could I. I actually didn't mind the classes, but it left me feeling kind of hollow inside. You know what I mean?"

Maisie nodded. "That's how you know it wasn't right. I've been there too."

MJ looked up. "Really?"

"Oh, yes. My parents wanted me to do law, like them." She rolled her eyes. "Both lawyers. But I went to theatre school instead."

MJ whistled. "I never knew you were an actress. I thought you did costume design."

"I majored in costume design, but I also enjoyed stomping the boards." She chuckled at the memory. "Anyway, they accepted it in the end."

"Especially when you got a job in Hollywood," MJ added.

"That didn't hurt."

MJ paused for a moment.

"I'm thinking about going to fashion design college," she said, after a beat.

"Oh, that's a wonderful idea!" Maisie nodded enthusiastically. "You're so creative, I can see you doing something like that."

"I feel like I'm not good enough," she said, pouting.

"Nobody is when they start out," Maisie said, reaching over to pat her hand. "That's why you go to school. To learn."

MJ gave a tentative nod. "True."

"It's what you make of yourself, that's important."

"Thanks, Maisie," MJ said, brightening. "That helps."

A customer walked in the door and looked around to see if anyone was around to help.

"Good. Now do you want to help me fold this material?"

MJ grinned. "Of course."

By midafternoon, the store had quietened again. The flurry of customers had been good for business, but Maisie was ready for a sit down and a cup of tea. The coffee had made her jittery, and she found her thoughts circling back to Harvey, and of course, Margot.

MJ had left for her shift at the diner and Mewsly still hadn't returned, so she had the store to herself.

She was just getting comfortable in the rocker with the most recent edition of Cross Stitch, when she heard a tap on the glass. Glancing up, she saw Deputy Andy standing outside.

"Hi, come on in," she said, opening the door. He was dressed smartly in his deputy uniform, his hands on his hips.

"I'm afraid this isn't a social call, Maisie. I have some news that I think you're going to want to hear."

"Oh?" She waved him in anyway, a feeling of dread growing in the pit of her stomach. She could tell by his expression that this wasn't good. "What is it?"

He stepped into the store and faced her.

"We recovered the remains," he told her.

"Oh! But that's good news." She frowned as he flattened his lips into a straight line. "Isn't it?"

"Not exactly."

"Why? Wasn't there enough DNA left for a confirmation? Did you find any clues as to who'd buried him?"

Andy held up a hand. "Slow down," he cautioned. "The remains were in a very poor condition. It looked like the wild animals had gotten to them. There was also substantial decay."

Maisie bit her lip. "And?"

"They're still with the medical examiner," he hedged, "but that's not what I wanted to tell you."

"What then?"

"We've arrested someone in connection with the disappearance."

She gasped. "You found something? Fiber, trace evidence? A personal item that led to the kidnapper?"

"Not exactly. But we have a man in custody. He was questioned in relation to the abduction at the time."

Maisie's heart sank. "Who is it?"

But she knew. She knew before he'd even said the words.

There was a brief silence.

"Jed Sutter."

Maisie gripped the steering wheel as she drove to the sheriff's department for the second time that week.

Dread coiled in her stomach and she felt slightly nauseous. Although, that could be the copious amounts of coffee she'd drunk today.

Poor Jed.

The one thing he'd feared had come true.

They'd promised anonymity, and now he was being questioned. She couldn't help but feel responsible.

Maisie parked, got out of the car, and marched inside.

Deputy Andy wasn't there. He'd gone on somewhere else after coming to speak to her, but he'd asked her not to tell the sheriff that he'd been there. He'd only told her as a courtesy.

She appreciated that, but now she had to speak to Markham. Make him see that Jed was one of the good guys. That he'd come forward with the information because it had been the right thing to do.

That he wasn't involved in baby Tobias's disappearance.

Markham stood in the center of the room with a coffee in one hand, a donut in the other. Really? He was eating donuts and he had a man in custody.

She sucked in a breath.

"Sheriff, I need to speak to you about Jed Sutter."

He leveled her with a look. "Ms. Button, this has nothing to do with you."

She spluttered at that. "Actually, it has everything to do with me. I was the one who spoke to Jed and convinced him to share what he knew. He's here because of me."

And Cherry, but that wasn't the point.

"Thank you for your contribution," he said dryly. "But the man lives in the area where the remains were found. Plus, he was a suspect in the original investigation."

"That doesn't mean he's guilty," she argued, only just keeping her temper in check.

"When we picked him up, he confessed to having told you the location of the remains," the sheriff said, albeit reluctantly. "This is protocol. I wouldn't be doing my job if I didn't question him."

Maisie stared at him. Okay, that did kind of make sense.

"He didn't do it," she whispered.

"That's not for me to decide."

Down the corridor, a door opened and one of the other deputies who Maisie didn't know, stepped into the hallway.

She gasped as he was followed by Jed.

Somehow, he looked older and more fragile than he had at the cabin. With his wild hair and rugged appearance, he appeared totally out of place in the sheriff's office.

"Don't leave town," Sheriff Markham told him as he walked past. "We might need to speak to you again."

Jed stopped. "Where would I go?"

With a curt nod to Maisie, Markham and his donut disappeared down the hall to his office.

Maisie hurried over to Jed. "I'm so sorry," she said, her heart twisting in her chest. "We didn't mean for your name to get out. We only ever gave the sheriff the coordinates."

Jed shook his head. "They came looking, like I knew they would. Didn't seem much point in keeping it a secret since they were questioning me anyway."

They walked slowly toward the door. "What did they ask you?"

"He wanted to know where I was last week. If I'd spoken to a woman, someone who died."

"Margot?"

He nodded. "And another fella too. Can't remember the name."

"Harvey Dillard?" she guessed.

"That's the one." Jed gave a dry chuckle. "Deputy asked me what vehicle I drove. Told them I haven't gotten behind the wheel since the Carter administration."

Maisie smiled, despite herself. They came to a stop outside.

"How do you get food?" she asked. "I mean, I know Irma brings you supplies, but that's only once a month."

"I get what I need from the farmers' markets. A guy out near Fern Ridge gave me half a hog the other day. Turns out it was the same day as your friend died."

Maisie couldn't mask her relief. "So you've got an alibi."

"Seems so," Jed muttered. "Sheriff said he was gonna check."

The sun chose that moment to break through and they felt the warmth on their backs. Maisie took it to be a sign.

Then, the door to the sheriff's department opened and Markham strode out. He had a strange look on his face, like he was confused about something.

"Ms. Button," he called. "Wait there."

She stopped.

"Are they gonna arrest me?" Jed asked.

"I don't think it's you," Maisie whispered as the sheriff strode toward them.

"That was the ME on the phone," he began, then paused to catch his breath. "I thought you should know, the remains Rutherford Timber retrieved from the woods—"

She nodded eagerly. They'd found something, some clue that would exonerate Jed and lead them to the real killer.

"They were female."

Maisie stared at him as his words landed.

"It was a little girl?" Jed muttered, running a hand over his head.

The sheriff turned to face him. "Yeah. You didn't find Tobias Hollowell."

Maisie's mind reeled. "Then, whose remains did Jed find?"

Chapter 21

Button Therapy

"You mean it wasn't Tobias?" Brian asked, pausing in the middle of a row. The little jacket he was knitting for one of his dachshunds was finally taking shape.

"No," Maisie said, leaning back in her chair, her own knitting abandoned on the table. "They don't know who it is."

Brian frowned. "But they were human?"

"I believe so. Female," she told him.

"Holy moly," whispered Ree, shaking her head. "This is getting very confusing."

"Tell me about it," Bev nodded.

The circle had gathered as usual, but this evening, Maisie detected a need for community and comfort, rather than sleuthing. Harvey's death and Jed's arrest had shocked them all, and they had gravitated together to process.

"At least Jed is off the hook," Cherry said, reaching for her hot chocolate. Nobody had opted for coffee tonight.

"Yes, thankfully," Maisie agreed.

"I still haven't spoken to Father—" She broke off as a figure appeared at the door. It was Jesse, and he was carrying an enormous bunch of pink roses.

Maisie glanced at MJ, who'd gone very still.

"I think that's for you," she said, masking a smile.

MJ got up and walked over to the door.

"Can I come in?" Jesse asked, taking off his cap with the Sycamore Hills Golf Estate logo on.

She glanced at the flowers, and then over at Maisie. "Um, sure. I guess."

Maisie nodded, and MJ stepped back to let him in. "These are for you," he said, handing her the roses.

"Oh, how lovely," Ree breathed.

"It's to say sorry, for standing you up."

"Aw," murmured Cherry, who was a romantic at heart. El gazed at Jesse with wide eyes, while Mewsly narrowed hers suspiciously.

"I thought I owed you an explanation." He glanced over at the table where everyone was watching him, then back at MJ. "I'd really like to explain, if you'll let me."

She glanced down at the roses in her hand. "Okay."

He broke into a relieved smile. "Great."

"If you want some privacy," Maisie said, "you can go into my office at the back."

"That's okay. I think you need to hear this too, Maisie. Since it was you who came to my rescue."

Maisie nodded. That much was true, and she wanted to know where he'd been the night Harvey was murdered. It might make the picture a little clearer.

"Come and sit down, dear," Ree said, gesturing to a free chair around the table.

He hesitated, but only for moment, then sat down, placing his cap on the table.

"I'll put those in some water," Bev said, getting up. MJ hadn't moved from the doorway. "You sit down."

MJ sat on the other end of the table to Jesse. She wasn't going to make this easy on him.

"Did you just come from the golf course?" Maisie asked, to start things off.

"Yes, but I'm done for the day now."

He glanced at MJ and cleared his throat. "You all know about my dad, right?"

Maisie nodded.

"He ran out on you when you were a kid, didn't he?" Cherry said with a frown. She knew first-hand what that was like.

"Yeah. Well, the night of our date, he called me."

MJ gasped. "Why didn't you tell me? I'd have understood."

"He wanted to meet up," Jesse continued, shifting in his chair. "I didn't want to see him. I mean, it's been so long, and what he did—"

Cherry had tensed, the muscles in her neck popping. "That's totally understandable."

"That's why I didn't say anything. I wasn't going to go."

"You changed your mind?" Maisie asked, gently.

"He called again. Said he really wanted to speak to me. I decided to give him an hour. That's it. One hour to state his case, and then I was going to leave and pick you up."

MJ nodded, her face softer now.

"What happened?" Ree asked.

"I went to meet him at the bar, but he wasn't there."

"He didn't show?" MJ asked, outraged.

Cherry just shook her head. "Leopard never changes its spots."

"I waited, then called him. He didn't answer. Finally, he sent me a text message, saying he couldn't do it. That I was better off without him in my life." He paused. "It really messed me up."

Cherry looked like she was about to strangle someone.

"I'm so sorry," Maisie whispered.

"That sucks," Eloise chimed in.

"It sure does," Brian agreed.

"Anyway, I hung around for a while, thinking about it. Trying to understand why he didn't want to see me."

"He doesn't deserve you," Cherry blurted out.

Ree nodded in agreement.

"Then I left. But I was distracted and not looking where I was going. I hit what I thought was a pothole—"

Everybody cringed.

"Which I now know was Harvey lying in the street."

Ree let out a shaky breath. The thought was too terrible to contemplate.

"And then I went home." He stared across at MJ. "I was too upset to go on a date. I didn't want to let you down, so I didn't do anything. I feel really bad about it."

MJ jumped up, walked around the table and to his surprise, wrapped her arms around him. "It's okay. I get it. Your father is a jerk. You don't need him."

Maisie smiled at Ree as they hugged.

Brian put his hands together and sighed.

"I'm sorry that happened to you," Maisie said, after the poignant moment had passed. "But thank you for sharing with us."

"I hope you won't judge me," he said, but he was looking at MJ.

"Not at all," she said firmly. "We'll just have to go on an even better date to make up for it."

He broke into a wide grin. "I was hoping you'd say that."

"You've had a long day," Ree said, pushing herself up. "Let me make you some hot chocolate. You look like you need it."

He nodded gratefully. "That would be great. I didn't get a chance to eat at the resort before I left. There was a kind of funny vibe there, actually."

"Oh?" Maisie looked up. "What kind of vibe?"

"Everyone was on edge about something. The landscaper had messed up and Mr. Penrose was angry with the company. Not me," he added hastily.

Maisie let out a disappointed breath. She'd been hoping for something more substantial.

"Anyway, on my way out, I saw Mrs. Penrose behind the clubhouse. She was standing by herself, crying."

Bev frowned. "June Penrose was crying?"

"I didn't know she had emotions," Cherry murmured.

Brian snorted.

"Do you know what had upset her?" Maisie asked, frowning. Something played at the corners of her mind but she couldn't quite grasp it.

"No, sorry. I didn't ask, either. I just walked past her to my truck and left."

Suddenly, Maisie knew what had been bugging her about June. The evening Harvey had died. In the bakery. She'd been coming out as Maisie gone in. They'd nearly collided in the doorway.

She massaged her temples. No, that wasn't it. June had

been perfectly pleasant then. Polite even. Nothing had seemed off.

Not with her.

But Harvey... Tired, distracted. Making mistakes with orders.

"What's going on in your head?" Cherry asked, studying her. "You've thought of something, haven't you?"

"Do you know what upset June?" MJ asked.

Maisie blinked and looked up at her friends. "I think I do."

Chapter 22

A Warped Truth

I t was time to complete the tapestry.

With everything that had happened lately, Maisie hadn't looked at it in days. Not properly. It was always there, in the back of the store, its presence unavoidable, but she'd stopped studying the details so intensely.

Navigating past button jars, baskets of yarn, and dangling displays of craft kits and thread, she steered the towering loom toward the farmhouse table. The sun fell on the textured surface, causing the red, gold and copper threads to glow with a life of their own.

Then there was the unfinished bit. The rows at the top that she hadn't completed yet. It had seemed like a gargantuan undertaking, but time was running out. The anniversary was approaching, and the mayor wanted a completed design with which to commemorate it.

Last night, after Jesse's dramatic confession, she'd watched a lengthy YouTube video on weaving. Now she had a much better idea of what she had to do.

Positioning a chair in front of it, she took a deep breath. No biggie.

How hard could it be?

One inch of plain background, then a straight, clean top border. She could do this.

Tapestry weaving, Maisie had discovered, was vastly different to sewing or crocheting. Especially on a large loom like Margot's.

The tall, beautifully crafted wooden frame was what was known in the industry as high warp, meaning the tapestry hung vertically in front of the weaver as it progressed. Two beams, one top and one bottom, supported the canvas.

There was a foot pedal at the base called a treadle, which controlled the threads' movement, not unlike a vintage sewing machine.

Maisie ran her finger along the edge. The vertical threads were "warp," forming the bones of the design. The horizontal ones were "weft," woven through using small, pointed wooden tools called shuttles. Each color had its own shuttle, and when not in use, they dangled from their threads like a colorful waterfall.

Tying her hair up, she grasped the shuttle wrapped in gold thread and began. Gold first. Then brown. Then another strip of gold. And so she wove.

An hour passed. Then another. She paused only to stretch and serve the occasional customer, proudly showing off the tapestry when anyone asked.

Slowly but surely, she found her rhythm.

The work was slow going, but therapeutic. With each

line of thread pressed snugly into place by the treadles, she felt herself syncing with the loom's soft creaks and the subtle tug of thread through her fingers.

Unable to help it, she began to think about the clues stitched into the fabric.

The church with the upside-down cross.

The small figure in the flames.

The initials *TH* etched into the borders.

The sycamore tree, standing where the oak should be.

She thought about how far they'd come. The sycamore had led them to Sycamore Hills Golf Estate. The flames and initials had pointed them to the truth about baby Tobias. Yet the puzzle remained unfinished.

The tapestry stopped just short of naming who had done it. Who had stolen Tobias. Who had killed Margot. Who may have killed Harvey.

She stared again at the church with the upside-down cross. Was it meant to be a sign of corruption? A literal church? A person connected to the church?

Then there was Father Tom Butterfield. She hadn't gone back to see him yet, because she hadn't known what to ask. She still didn't.

She couldn't outrightly accuse the church of altering the land documents. It was so long ago, anyway. Who would believe her?

On she weaved until a soft scraping at the door made her glance up. Mewsly stared back at her, tail curling around her paws.

Goodness, was that the time?

She got up and opened the door, letting her tabby in who made a beeline for her bowl, only to realize it wasn't there.

Turning, she looked up at Maisie expectantly.

"Yes, yes. I know."

She fed Mewsly early, before she locked up for the day, otherwise she got grumpy. And a hangry tabby was not a good thing.

Maisie prepared her food, but as she bent to set the bowl on the floor, she spotted a crumb stuck to Mewsly's whisker.

Realization dawned. "Oh, my gosh! You are such a faker," she told her cat. "You've been having double dinners, haven't you?"

And then it hit her. Like a lightning bolt to the brain.

She finally realized what Margot had been trying to tell them. Slowly, she turned to look back at the tapestry. At the burning figure in the flames. At the initials. At the sycamore. And finally, at the upside-down cross.

"Oh my god," she whispered. "That has to be it."

By the time the Knit and Natter group arrived that evening, Maisie had completed the tapestry. It had taken all day. Far longer than the three-hour promise of any tutorial she'd watched. But now, as the group began filing in, she stood proudly beside the loom, ready to unveil the final result.

"Presenting..." she announced, unable to wait for everyone to sit down. "Margot's tapestry!"

Stepping aside, she revealed the completed piece still hanging taut in the loom's warp threads.

"Wow, great job!" Cherry exclaimed, one arm still in her coat sleeve. Eloise gave a delighted cry and rushed over to take a closer look.

"Well done," Brian boomed, while Ree clasped Maisie's hand.

"You did it," she said, eyes sparkling. "And it looks wonderful."

"It really does," agreed MJ.

"Margot would be proud," Bev added warmly. "Now the town will get to see her work—and remember her for it."

Maisie fought back tears. "I hope so."

"Of course," Ree seconded.

Maisie used the time it took for them to settle around the table to compose herself. Once everyone had a beverage, and were seated comfortable, she cleared her throat.

"That's not all the news I've got."

"There's more?" Ree asked.

"You've figured it out, haven't you?" Cherry guessed.

"You have?" Brian shook his head.

"How?" MJ asked.

She laughed and held up a hand. "One at a time. Firstly, yes. I think I may have figured it out. I'm not a hundred percent yet, but I'm close."

"You know who killed Margot?" Brian asked.

"And Harvey."

They all glanced at each other.

"And I think I know who kidnapped Tobias Hollowell."

There was a stunned silence.

Eloise spoke first. "You solved the puzzle."

She nodded at the teen. "I need to check some details first, but yes. I believe I have."

"What details?" Bev demanded. "Can we help?"

Maisie grinned. "I was hoping you'd ask that."

While they listened, she explained what she needed.

"Bev, did you know the sheriff who worked the Hollowell case?"

"Wyden?" Bev scoffed. "I didn't work with him, but I knew him."

"Is he still alive?"

"Oh, yes. Lives in a retirement home now. What do you need?"

"Could you ask him a couple of questions for us?"

"Of course. I forgot he was still around, not that he'll be of much use. He wasn't much back then, either."

Brian smirked.

Next, she turned to Cherry. "Do you think you could stop by Rutherford Timber?"

"Of course. What do you need?"

"A map. One they should have in their archives."

Cherry's brow lifted in interest.

Maisie continued, "Harriet won't mind. She knows we went hiking out that way."

"Let me guess," Brian folded his arms in front of his body, "you want a map of the forest as it was back then?"

Maisie grinned. "1984. Exactly."

"I'll have it by tomorrow evening," Cherry promised.

"When are you going to tell us who the murderer is?" Eloise wanted to know.

"Tomorrow," Maisie promised. "I've decided to host a little gathering. Share what we've found with all those involved."

"A final reveal!" Eloise clapped her hands together.

Maisie glanced at Cherry, then back to Eloise. "I'm sorry, honey. I'm not sure it's appropriate material for kiddos."

Eloise's face fell. "Aw, come on. I'm nearly twelve."

But Cherry nodded in agreement. "You've been wanting to have dinner at Lila's house for ages, right?"

Her face brightened. "Yeah, but it's a school night."

"I'll call Lila's mom and ask her if she minds," Cherry finished.

Eloise looked torn.

"Fine," she said, turning back ot her book. "But only if you promise to fill me in on all the gory details."

Cherry smiled. "I promise."

"Well, this all sounds very intriguing," Ree interjected, bringing them back to the topic at hand. "Any jobs for me?"

Maisie broke into a smile. "I was hoping you'd ask. There are a few people I'd like to invite, and I'd love your help reaching out to them."

She handed Ree a short guest list. Ree scanned it, her eyes gleaming.

"What about me?" Brian asked, as MJ tried to peer over Ree's shoulder at the list.

"I'll need copies of some historical records. I'll text you the details."

"Roger that." He gave a firm nod.

MJ looked up. "Am I the only one without a task?"

"Nope. Could you handle snacks? I won't have time tomorrow."

"Absolutely," MJ agreed. "What are you going to do?"

"I need to speak to Father Tom," she said. "I finally know what it is I want to ask him."

"This is so exciting," Eloise murmured, cheeks flushed. "I can't wait to hear what happens."

Maisie smiled. "Me too, kiddo. Me too."

In her lunch hour the following day, Maisie locked the store and walked across town to St. Paul's Episcopal Church.

It was a perfect spring afternoon. The sky was blue, the air was filled with the sweet scent of cherry blossom and sunlight warmed her back as she walked through Founders Park.

Despite the beautiful day, a nervous anticipation stirred in her belly. She tried to ignore it but found herself worrying the ruby ring on her right hand as she walked.

If her theory was right, and if Cherry and Bev came back with the confirmation she needed, then she'd have the final pieces of the puzzle. It would all finally make sense.

Baby Tobias's disappearance. Margot's murder. Harvey's death.

She found Father Tom in his vestry, a small room accessible by an exterior door around the side of the church.

"Maisie," he said, looking up. "This is a surprise. What can I do for you?"

She closed the door behind her and turned to face him. "Father Tom. I need your help."

He frowned. "Of course. Why don't you sit down and tell me?"

She took a seat, squared her shoulders, and told him what she needed.

Twenty minutes later, Maisie emerged from the cool church into the warmth of the afternoon.

As the church door shut behind her, she stood for a moment on the stone path, taking deep breaths and trying to still her racing heart.

Finally, she had all the answers.

It had been there, all along, staring them in the face. They just hadn't been asking the right questions.

And tonight, she would share them with everyone.

Chapter 23

The Final Picture

Maisie could not wait for six o'clock.

She was sorting out the button drawer when her phone pinged. It was a message from Bev.

Finally.

Heart thumping, she scanned it.

Yes!

Nodding at Mewsly curled tightly in her basket by the yarn display, she said, "It's exactly as I thought, Mews. Everything's coming together."

The tabby, who'd just finished an extended grooming session, wasn't interested in this announcement. Yawning, she closed her eyes and went back to sleep.

Maisie, however, couldn't sit still. As a result, the rest of the day passed painfully slowly.

After reorganized the thread display again, and placing

an order for too much fabric, she took to pacing around the store.

Brian provided a brief respite when he called and confirmed he had the documents she'd asked for.

"You were right," he murmured into the phone. "See you later."

There was only one more person to invite.

Taking a deep breath, she placed a call to Sheriff Markham.

"If you've got a lead for me, Ms. Button," he growled, "give it to me straight and I'll investigate."

"I don't have a lead," Maisie replied. "I have the truth. Margot Bellamy and Harvey Dillard's killer will be at my store tonight. Six o'clock sharp."

That got his attention.

"Fine," he said, after a long pause. "I'll be there. But just so we're clear, I don't encourage vigilantism. You and your little circle of friends should not be prying into sheriff's business."

"We'd never do anything reckless," Maisie assured him, wondering if the hike to Jed Sutter's cabin qualified. "But we consider it our civic duty to share what we've discovered, and we wanted you to be the first to know."

He grunted. "See you later."

Six o'clock arrived at last.

Maisie had set the stage and was ready for the final act. The overhead lights were switched off, leaving only the warm glow of the lamps, which cast a soft light over the room and drew the eye straight to Margot's tapestry.

The coffee maker gurgled away steadily, filling the air

with its rich aroma, and enough chairs had been positioned around the farmhouse table to cater for everyone.

Then for the pièce de résistance. Margot's finished tapestry, mounted on the tall wooden loom, was positioned at the head of the table where it could not be missed.

Only Mewsly remained untouched by the sense of occasion, fast asleep in her basket, unaware of the quiet anticipation gathering around her.

MJ arrived first with trays of snacks. She arranged them on the table, along with a pile of napkins, and breathed a sigh of relief.

"That should keep everyone busy for a while."

"Thank you," Maisie shot her a grateful smile.

"How are you feeling?" MJ asked.

"Nervous but determined to put on a good show."

"Your theatrical experience will come in useful," MJ observed with a grin.

That it would.

Cherry arrived next but without her daughter. Eloise had successfully been deposited at Lila's house for their once-in-a-blue-moon school-night playdate.

"She couldn't be happier." Cherry handed Maisie a print-out of a large map. "This is what you wanted."

She scanned the layout. Yep, that was exactly what she was looking for.

"Perfect," she whispered, pressing the map to her chest.

Ree and Bev arrived together, followed by Brian with a slim stack of records tucked under one arm. He nodded at Maisie, before taking a seat at the table.

Sheriff Markham marched in a short while later, accompanied by Deputy Andy who sat as far away as possible to Jesse Turner, who'd arrived just before him.

Father Tom shuffled in looking nervous, along with a

smiling Mayor Greg Penrose and his parents, June and William Penrose.

"What a charming place," June said, giving the store an appraising glance. William gave an agreeable nod and went to greet the sheriff and Mayor Penrose, but he stopped in front of the tapestry instead.

"Now *this* must be the long-awaited tapestry. How spectacular. A worthy addition to our anniversary."

"It truly is amazing," the major added, not to be outdone.

"Maisie finished it," Bev clarified.

"A worthy effort."

The door jingled and in walked Harriet Rutherford and her husband. Maisie went over to greet her. "Thank you for coming."

"I'm intrigued," she said, nodding at June Penrose.

The last to arrive were Lynda and Glynis. They'd come together, but both looked nervous, their faces pinched with tension.

"Please, take a seat," Maisie told them, gesturing to the semi-circle of chairs. They nodded and shuffled over. Maisie noticed June Penrose give them a hard stare, before turning away again.

Cherry leaned over and whispered in Maisie's ear. "Wow, talk about setting the stage."

MJ winked at her.

The performance was about to begin.

"Thank you for coming tonight," Maisie announced, standing at the head of the table, beside the loom. "I invited you here tonight to celebrate the completion of Margot's tapestry, and to thank you for helping me finish it. Every one of you offered some insight into the design of this work of art."

There was a polite ripple of applause.

"I, for one, was happy to contribute," June Penrose said.

Maisie smiled at her.

"What you all may not know, is that Margot's tapestry depicts far more than images of Thistle Grove. It contains clues, hidden messages about a secret that's been buried for a very long time."

Mayor Penrose frowned. "Do we have to bring this up now? I thought I'd made myself clear. No mention of the Hollowells, or the town's tragic past."

"This is not just about that," Maisie corrected. "It's also about Margot's and Harvey Dillard's murder."

He frowned. "I don't understand."

"You really didn't want Margot to put those symbols in there, did you?" Maisie said, turning to him.

He spread his hands. "You know I didn't."

"So much so that at first I thought you might be willing to kill to stop her."

"Hey, wait a moment," William interrupted, scrambling to his feet.

June had turned puce. "How dare you!"

Before the mayor could object, Maisie continued, "But of course, you didn't. You're not a killer."

The mayor's shoulders relaxed. "At least we're clear on that."

With a huff, William retook his seat.

The sheriff was watching her intently, as was Andy, coffee mug poised mid-sip.

"Except some secrets are impossible to keep buried." Maisie turned to look across the table. "Isn't that right, Father?"

Father Tom shifted in his seat. "I don't know what you mean," he mumbled.

"Yes, you do. Margot found out about the inconsistencies in the church property records, didn't she? That's why she weaved an inverted cross into the tapestry. She knew the church had undercut the Rutherfords all those years ago."

"Before my time," Father Tom muttered.

"What's this?" William snapped.

"I'm afraid it's true," Harriet cut in, glancing across at William. "I studied the documents myself. There are clear inconsistencies."

"I didn't know about this," William ran a hand through his thinning hair.

"None of us did," Harriet conceded. "It was a long time ago, which is why I've decided not to do anything about it."

Maisie smiled at her. "That is very gracious of you, Harriet."

"The town was built on those foundations," Harriet continued, glancing around the group. "Unsettling them now can bring no good."

There were several nods of agreement.

"I still want to see evidence of this," William grunted.

Harriet nodded. "We will get together later and discuss it, but somehow, I don't think that is the reason we are here."

She looked back to Maisie.

"You're right. At first we thought maybe Father Tom had murdered Margot to keep her quiet about the fraud."

Father Tom opened his mouth to protest, but Maisie raised her hand, cutting him off. "We now know that's not true. There's a far more sinister reason."

June's eyes snapped to her, uneasy.

"I thought this was a celebration?" Mayor Penrose said.

"It's a lot more than that." Maisie shifted her gaze from Father Tom to the Penroses. "Margot left clues in the tapestry, but I didn't understand them until now."

"What clues?" William demanded, his gaze shifting to the tapestry.

"Apart from the inverted cross, there was the fire and the baby in the flames," Maisie pointed out. "It was only when I questioned Father Tom that he told me the truth."

June swung around to confront the priest. "You didn't?"

"Mother?" Mayor Penrose turned to June. "Didn't what?"

William was still staring at the tapestry. "What truth?"

But June folded her arms tightly and said nothing. Both Lynda and Glynis shifted in their seats.

"Margot uncovered something other than the fraudulent land deeds when she was looking through the church records at St. Paul's. She found Tobias Hollowell's birth certificate."

"So what?" William demanded. "He was registered at the church."

"She also discovered his death certificate."

Lynda hung her head.

The sheriff frowned. "I thought he was abducted."

"The death certificate was for the stillborn child born to June and William Penrose."

Gasps rippled through the room. Glynis put a hand on Lynda's arm.

"No, you've got that wrong," William protested. "Greg is our son."

June had gone white now. She sat as if turned to stone, her gaze burning into Maisie.

"June?" her husband asked.

Maisie cocked her head. "Would you like to tell them? Or should I?"

"You go right ahead," June snapped. "Since you seem to know everything anyway."

Maisie bowed her head. "I'm sorry, June, but it's time for the truth to come out."

June lifted her chin, a small gesture of defiance. "Nothing you say will change anything."

She was wrong there. It would change everything.

Maisie took a breath. "In 1984, June gave birth to a still-born baby. A little girl."

William clutched the table, his knuckles white. "What?"

Maisie nodded. "It's true, we have the records to prove it. She didn't tell anyone aside from her midwife. The shame must have been too great. Or perhaps she hadn't wanted people's pity."

"A baby girl?" Penrose repeated. He stared at his mother, face crumpled in confusion. "When?"

June didn't reply.

Maisie turned to her. "It happened the night before the Hollowells' garden party, didn't it? Unable to face what had happened, you showed up at that party pretending to still be pregnant."

A stunned silence settled on the room. All eyes were on June.

"You must have been devasted," Maisie said, gently. "Is that why you concealed it?"

"You can't even imagine," June muttered. Her eyes glistened, but she tightened her mouth and looked away.

"I don't think you planned what happened next," Maisie said. "I think it was grief, and pain, and desperation. You saw an opportunity and you took it."

Lynda had her hands over her mouth and was staring, stunned, at June.

Maisie continued. "Lynda left Baby Tobias alone in the nursery, taking his nap. You said you were feeling unwell, and you slipped away—but not before you snuck into Tobias's room and smuggled him off the property."

Lynda gasped audibly. "That was you? All these years... I thought it was my fault for leaving him. I blamed myself."

June glared at her. "It *was* your fault. You left him unattended."

"Don't you dare speak to her that way," Glynis cut in. "Not after what you've done."

William was staring at his wife like he didn't know who she was. Maisie couldn't blame him. To find out your wife had lied about something so important for all these years... It must be devastating.

"You told me you'd delivered the baby on your own," he said in a strangled whisper.

Penrose turned to Maisie, the penny finally dropping.

"Are you saying that I'm not—" He couldn't finish. Pain flashed across his handsome features.

Ree, who was sitting closest, laid a hand on his arm.

"Tobias Hollowell didn't disappear," Maisie continued. "He's right here in this room. Greg, you're actually the son of Ada and Robert Hollowell."

There was a shocked murmur.

Sheriff Markham stiffened, his gaze slanting to June. Deputy Andy still hadn't drunk his coffee.

Penrose faced his mother. "Is it true? Did you steal me?"

June didn't flinch.

"I rescued you," she corrected.

"Oh God." William dropped his head into his hands. "What have you done?"

"I rescued him," she repeated. "That woman didn't care about him. She passed him off to a nanny, and even she left him unattended. It was neglect. I did him a favor by taking him."

"Ada Hollowell was a loving mother," Bev corrected. "We've spoken to people who knew her. She adored her son."

"Oh, really?" June snapped. "You knew her, did you? Were you there, Beverley? Funny, because I don't recall seeing you at the garden party."

Bev sighed. MJ touched her arm and shook her head.

June got to her feet, eyes flashing. "I was at that party. I saw Ada. Laughing, drinking champagne while her baby was left alone. Yes, I had a stillbirth. You can't know what that was like. I was alone. Just me and the midwife." She turned on her husband. "You were at work. You were always working. You had no idea what I was going through."

William, speechless, could only shake his head.

"What about the midwife?" the sheriff asked. "Why didn't she speak up?"

"I made her promise not to say anything. I paid her to keep quiet. She needed the money."

"Except, you didn't know she'd filed a death certificate," Maisie pointed out.

June's chest rose and fell. "Obviously, not."

Cherry gasped. "You buried your baby in the woods?"

June's head snapped toward her. "How did you—?"

"We found the remains," Deputy Andy said, finally pulling himself together. "We found her last week."

A strange stillness passed over June's face. "It was peaceful there, surrounded by trees."

William made a strangled sound.

"Don't judge me," she said to her husband. "That was the hardest thing I'd ever done."

"Until a few weeks ago," Maisie continued, "when Margot came to ask about the death certificate she found, and the fact that there was no record of Greg's birth."

"He didn't *need* a birth certificate," June sniffed. "Not until he turned sixteen and wanted his driver's license. It was easy to forge, if you know the right people."

"Margot figured it out," Maisie continued. "She put the pieces together. She knew Greg Penrose was really Tobias Hollowell. That's when you panicked."

MJ turned to June. "You broke into her home in the middle of the night and stabbed her!"

"Nonsense," June snapped. "Of course I didn't."

Sheriff Markham's hand drifted toward the cuffs at his belt, but Maisie wasn't finished.

"There was a witness," she said. "Harvey Dillard was awake early that morning, baking. He saw you coming out of Margot's house, didn't he?"

"He was at the bakery every morning before dawn," Cherry confirmed.

Maisie fixed her gaze on June. "When you realized that, you knew he had to die. He could identify you."

"It's all rubbish," June scoffed, glancing at her husband.

"You lured him somewhere quiet," Maisie continued, ignoring her. "You struck him from behind, then left his body in the street to make it look like an accident."

MJ's voice trembled with anger. "Poor Jesse thought he'd killed Harvey."

Jesse looked ashen. "I was arrested and nearly charged with manslaughter."

June stared at him. "Maybe you did do it. You can't prove otherwise."

"You had the means, the motive, and the opportunity," Bev said coolly. Sheriff Markham arched an eyebrow but said nothing.

June's gaze swept the room. "You all believe I did this? You believe I stabbed Margot with her own scissors, then murdered Harvey too?"

The mayor turned away in disgust.

Her husband, ashen-faced, attempted to rise but faltered and fell back down in his chair. "Those nights... my headaches... You were drugging me so you could sneak out and commit murder?"

It was phrased like a question, but the truth was clear in his haunted gaze.

June's face twisted. "Don't be absurd. I can't believe you think I'm capable of that. Taking a baby and giving him a good home, yes, but murder?" She scoffed. "Nonsense."

There was a heavy pause.

"We never made that detail public. Only the people who found the body knew what weapon was used," Sheriff Markham said quietly.

June blinked. Her mouth opened like a goldfish, then closed.

Markham got to his feet. "June Penrose, you're under arrest for the murders of Margot Bellamy and Harvey Dillard."

"Don't forget the kidnapping of Tobias Holloway," MJ added.

Deputy Andy stepped forward. "Ma'am, if you'll come with me." He reached for her arm.

"No!" she shrieked, jumping out of the way, but Deputy Andy grabbed her, swung her around, slipping on the cuffs.

"That was pretty cool," Cherry said, glancing at MJ.

"I hope you're happy," June spat at Maisie, her eyes

wild. "You've dragged my shame through the mud. Exposed me for what? The Hollowells are gone. I raised that boy with love. Gave him a good home."

"Stealing a baby isn't love," Ree said.

MJ nodded. "Neither was killing two innocent people to cover up your crimes."

"You know nothing," June snarled. "I gave Greg everything. Look what he's become. That is because of me. Because of us and who we are."

Greg looked like he was about to faint. All his previous confidence and self-assuredness had melted away in the face of this startling truth.

"I'm not your son," he croaked, his voice hoarse. "You stole me from a woman who spent the rest of her short life grieving. You did this for you."

"Don't you dare!" June roared. "I am your mother. I raised you. I made you who you are today. You owe all this to us."

William got up and headed for the door.

"You're responsible too," June shrieked after him. "If you hadn't wanted an heir so badly."

He kept walking, shoulders stooped.

"Ma'am." Deputy Andy led her out.

Markham lingered. Maisie handed him the printed map and the death certificate Brian had retrieved.

"This is the only hard evidence we have," she said. "I hope it helps."

He took it with a nod. "We have a confession, so we don't really need it."

Greg stood frozen to the spot.

"I'm sorry," Maisie said, gently.

He turned to her and looked like he was about to say something, then pivoted abruptly and left the shop.

For a long beat no one moved.

Mewsly stirred in her basket, stretched, and sauntered across the room towards the door.

"Well," Brian murmured, eventually. "That was definitely our most interesting meeting to date."

Maisie let out a shaky breath and collapsed into a chair.

"I didn't see that coming," Cherry admitted, looking at Maisie. "I don't know how you figured it all out."

"Margot did," MJ said quietly. "She knew the truth and wanted us to find it."

"She would've been proud of you," Ree added. "You finished her tapestry and got justice for her and Harvey."

Maisie blinked back tears as she glanced around at her friends.

"*We* got justice," she amended.

Chapter 24

Figuring Things Out

Maisie smiled around the table.

It was the first Knit and Natter meeting since June Penrose's arrest. The shock of what had happened was beginning to die down and life in Thistle Grove was getting back to normal.

"I, for one, am glad that's over," Ree said, pulling a skein of soft lilac yarn from her bag.

Bev nodded. "Reminds me of why I retired. Can't say I miss all that excitement."

"I'm just glad she's behind bars," MJ muttered, pouring them all a mug of coffee from a pot Maisie had just brewed.

"Hear, hear," agreed Cherry.

"I can't believe I missed it," Eloise said, looking up from the rocking chair she was lounging on, Mewsly on her lap purring contently. "Although I had a great time at Lila's."

"How's Jesse?" Ree asked MJ with a small grin.

"Much better now the blame is laid at someone else's feet," she replied. "I can't believe she was ready to pin that on him."

"It would have been the next person who drove along," Maisie said, shaking her head. "Poor Harvey."

Brian laid down a ball of blue yarn beside the cable-knit dog sweater. "She deserves everything she gets." MJ nodded.

Since her arrest, June had remained in custody. The judge had denied bail, citing her as a risk to both witnesses and public safety.

"I saw Mayor Penrose the other day." Bev glanced at them above her glasses. "He didn't talk to me, but I heard he's distanced himself from the whole thing. He claims not to have known about any of it."

"I believe him," Maisie said.

The others nodded in agreement.

"This won't do his career any good," Cherry predicted, reaching for her coffee cup. "I'll bet he won't stand for re-election."

"No great shakes," MJ added.

Brian snorted. "The anniversary is next week. He's going to unveil the tapestry then."

Yesterday, Ree and Bev had helped Maisie carefully cut down the tapestry and tie off the final threads. Maisie had delivered it to Town Hall herself. Penrose hadn't been there, of course. He was keeping a very low profile until this blew over.

"The general public will never know about the clues Margot weaved into it," Maisie mused.

"No, but they'll always be part of Thistle Grove's history, just like the Hollowell tragedy and everything else.

Margot made sure of that."

"I heard William Penrose put his house on the market," Ree said.

Maisie lifted an eyebrow. "He probably can't live with his wife's betrayal."

"Or the shame," Cherry added.

"I heard he's going to Florida," MJ put in. "Far away from this mess."

Not even Greg was speaking to him now. Maisie doubted if they'd ever reconcile. Not after what had happened.

"Andy told me the sheriff has reopened the Ada Hollowell case," MJ informed them.

Maisie glanced up. This was news to her. "That's great. The fire?"

"Yes. With June's arrest, they're looking into the possibility of arson."

"Oh, Lord." Ree let out a shaky breath. "Is there no end to that woman's wickedness?"

"Apparently not." MJ went back to her knitting.

Maisie supposed it wasn't a stretch to imagine she might've had a hand in that tragedy too. The Penroses had been powerful. Too powerful to be questioned back then.

"I have something to cheer us up," Maisie announced, getting up from the table. She ducked into the back room and returned with a tray of brownies. "My first attempt at recreating the last treat Margot brought to the group, if you'll remember."

Everybody oohed and aahed and dived in.

"Not bad," Cherry said, nodding.

"Good enough for a second," Brian decided.

From Eloise's lap, Mewsly opened one lazy green-gold eye but made no move to get up.

Maisie smiled. The new feeding routine was working. So was the tiny, engraved tag on the cat's collar. *Mewsly. Don't feed!*

A bit cheeky, perhaps, but effective. Mewsly hadn't loved having an extra accessory, but she was coming home hungrier, with no lingering crumbs on her whiskers.

"How's the permission on the access road coming on?" Maisie asked Ree. After learning about Jed Sutter's living conditions, the retired teacher had taken the issue straight to the senior center and rallied a small army.

Ree beamed. "It's been approved. My army of volunteers are fixing up his cabin as we speak. It was in an appalling state."

"Jed allowed you to do this?" Cherry asked, surprised.

"Well, he didn't say no," Ree chuckled.

Maisie laughed. "Well, what do you know!"

"Hey, I was wondering," MJ said. "Mind if I bring Jesse to our next meeting? He's learning to knit."

"He is? That's great!" Maisie suspected it was just so he could spend some more time with MJ. "Of course you can."

"I'm glad you gave him another chance, dear," Ree said, patting her arm.

MJ flushed. "Me too. He's a good guy, he's just... figuring things out."

"Like all of us." Cherry glanced at her daughter, nose deep in a book.

A quiet rhythm returned. Needles clicked. Mewsly snored. Coffee cooled. And for the first time in weeks, Maisie felt herself relax. At last, all was quiet in their little corner of Thistle Grove. Somehow, though, she doubted it would stay that way.

Ready for another mystery to solve? Click here to order book two, *A Stitch Too Far*, or by using the link below!
https://a.co/d/ohWOP9OI

Did you enjoy *The Deadly Tapestry*? Don't forget to leave a review to let us know your thoughts!
https://a.co/d/o2kWbHPt

Tangled Threads Mysteries

The Deadly Tapestry

A Stitch Too Far

Also by Ellie Webster

Tails of Maple Ridge

The Peanut Butter Twist

Paws and Prejudice

Canine Confidential

The Barbershop Showdown

Old Tricks, New Trouble

Tangled Threads Mysteries

The Deadly Tapestry

A Stitch Too Far

About the Author

Ellie Webster is the shared pen name for a small group of writers who adore all things cozy and mysterious. Set in small picturesque towns, Ellie's stories feature lovable amateur sleuths, loyal pets, and plenty of twists tucked between cups of coffee and community gossip. Expect warmth, wit, and a mystery that keeps you turning the pages long after lights-out.

Perfect for readers who enjoy a steaming mug beside them, a faithful cat or dog at their feet, and the comforting promise that justice (and a slice of pie) will always be served.

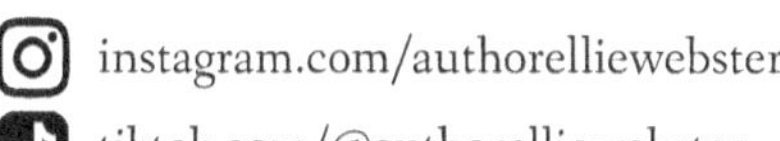

instagram.com/authorelliewebster
tiktok.com/@authorelliewebster

Join Ellie Webster's Newsletter

Follow the link to join our newsletter and stay up to date with upcoming releases, deals, and exclusive cozy content!

https://www.getdrip.com/forms/99805461/submissions/new